DOLL'S EYE

Leah Kaminsky is a physician and award-winning writer. Her debut novel, *The Waiting Room*, won the Voss Literary Prize. *The Hollow Bones* won both the Literary Fiction and Historical Fiction categories of the 2019 International Book Awards, and the 2019 American Book Fest's Best Book Award for Literary Fiction. Leah holds a Master of Fine Arts from Vermont College of Fine Arts, USA.

www.leahkaminsky.com

LEAH KAMINSKY

DOLL'S EYE

VINTAGE BOOKS
Australia

VINTAGE

UK | USA | Canada| Ireland | Australia
India | New Zealand | South Africa | China

Vintage is part of the Penguin Random House group of companies
whose addresses can be found at global.penguinrandomhouse.com.

Penguin
Random House
Australia

First published by Vintage, 2023

Cover image of landscape courtesy Claudia Holzforster/Arcangel; girl in dress courtesy
Aleshyn_Andrei/Shutterstock; worn suitcase courtesy Mylisa/Shutterstock;
fragments of old letters courtesy Arkady Mazor/Shutterstock.
Cover design by Debra Billson © Penguin Random House Australia Pty Ltd
Typeset in Adobe Garamond Pro by Midland Typesetters, Australia

Printed and bound in Australia by Griffin Press, an accredited
ISO AS/NZS 14001 Environmental Management Systems printer

A catalogue record for this
book is available from the
National Library of Australia

ISBN 978 1 76104 374 1

penguin.com.au

For Maia, Ella, Alon and Yohanan Loeffler

In memory of William Cooper (1860–1941), a Yorta Yorta man who, upon hearing of the events of Kristallnacht in Europe in 1938, was so outraged by the outburst of hatred and violence against Jews in Nazi Germany that he organised a march of First Nations peoples, leading a delegation to the German consulate in Melbourne. Cooper was turned away when he tried to present a letter condemning the persecution of Jews. This was among one of the first international protests against the atrocities perpetrated by Nazi Germany against the Jewish people.

Dos oyg is azoy kleyn, dokh zet es di gantse velt.
The eye is so small, yet it sees the entire world.

Yiddish proverb

Doll's Eye – a reflex used to determine
whether a patient is conscious.

AUTHOR'S NOTE

The locations in this work of fiction take place on country of the Yangman nation, the Jawoyn, Dagoman and Wardaman peoples and the Wurundjeri people of the Kulin nation. I respectfully acknowledge the Traditional Owners of these lands. First Nations peoples were the first storytellers here. I am grateful for their generous assistance in the writing of this work and thank them for welcoming me to Country. Sovereignty of this land has never been ceded.

PROLOGUE

CARLTON

1949

Anna Winter tore off her patient's head and lay it on the table. Tugging at the straw-like hair, she turned the head around. One eye stared back at her, blue and unblinking. Fishing some surgical pliers from the pocket of her starched laboratory coat, she pulled the lid of the other eye until it flipped open to reveal an empty crater. She ran her fingers over the pouty baby-face, fractured nose and rosebud mouth. Even though its body was battered and broken, Anna could see how much her patient had been loved. Cradling the cracked porcelain head, she dunked it into a tub of water. The remaining eye looked old, made of hand-blown glass. Luckily, it was still intact. Eyes like these would be difficult to replace.

'Her name's Betty.'

The client, her narrow lips pursed, stood on the other side of the table, like a student in the first row of an anatomy dissection. She stared owlishly at her beloved doll as Anna gently cleaned out the eye socket with a cotton swab. The raw-faced woman's life story began to ooze out.

'I've had her since I was four.' Her voice turned squeaky. 'That's sixty years.'

Anna glanced up.

'She was a gift from my nanna when Mother died.' A tear trickled down the woman's cheek. She explained the family dynamics, her dreadful marriage, her return to part-time work in a bakery after the children left home. As Anna listened to the litany of sorrows, she lay the doll's head back down and used a felt cloth to dry it carefully.

They all ended up telling her their stories; tragedies and joys spilled out into the chalice of her silence. There was the butcher's teddy bear, who had been left with him in a basket when he was abandoned on the doorstep of an orphanage as a newborn. Its smile had worn away over the years and he wanted it repaired. Or the toy soldier with a broken gun, belonging to a high-ranking bank official who carried it around in his briefcase for good luck. And every Friday morning the widow who lived up the street brought in her melancholy Raggedy Ann. Anna always helped lift the doll's mood by having a cup of tea and some home-baked biscuits with its owner. Tiny doll-souls absorbed everything, observing without seeing. A world of secrets stayed locked inside those eyes.

She reached for a box of glass orbs that rested beside her, each one cupped in its own small silken nest. They ranged in colour from greyish-green to blue and brown. She needed to get the eyes right. If they were disproportionate or had lids that blinked with an overly mechanical click, it made the doll look insensitive.

Choosing a blue eye for Betty that matched almost identically, Anna inserted it carefully into the socket. The customer, clutching her handbag, hovered closer. As the doll doctor slid the eye into place with a pair of forceps, the woman gasped:

'Don't hurt her!'

Anna flinched. The doll's eye suddenly slipped from her hand, clattering onto the floor, as though a flicker of life was ignited and it was trying to escape. The blue orb rolled away with the force of a marble and smashed against a metal shelf. They both watched in horror as it shattered into tiny shards.

Anna was not used to having someone watch her as she worked.

'Would you please leave?' she snapped with startling force, ushering the woman away with her free hand.

Betty's owner wiped a tear from her cheek and cleared her throat.

Anna feigned a smile and tried to soften her tone. 'If you would kindly come back later this afternoon, it would give me more time to pay closer attention to Betty. As you can see, it's a very delicate procedure.'

The woman picked up her handbag, straightened the front pleat of her skirt and scurried out of the shop. The bell tinkled as she closed the door behind her. Anna made a point of never asking how the damage to a doll had occurred. Most of the time clients would volunteer the gruesome details themselves, but Betty's owner, for all her babbling, had omitted the story of the doll's demise.

The workshop looked like a small amphitheatre, each wall lined with shelves that stretched all the way up to the ceiling. They held a galaxy of broken toys, some with disfigured faces, others suffering from unstrung limbs or missing teeth. The dolls ranged from expensive antique collector's items to those that merely looked like a dressed-up sock with limbs crudely moulded out of wax. A ceramic squirrel, missing a paw that once played a mandolin, leaned against a red-haired monkey smoking a broken pipe. A giraffe with a bent neck towered over a toy bishop who wore a torn cassock. Some of the dolls were hideous and beyond repair, black mould lining the edges of their pink mouths. Fixing each one involved a large degree of versatility and inventiveness. But repair always went far beyond the mere tinkering with a physical object. A true doll doctor restored the client's most treasured childhood memories. Discretion was meant to be paramount in Anna's profession, but this morning her patience had shattered along with the doll's eye.

People travelled to her from all over the country. Although there was no sign outside the workshop, those who sought her out seemed to somehow find their way instinctively to her door. Men would stand at the counter shuffling from one foot to the other, their cheeks reddening as they pulled moth-eaten toy dogs out from duffel bags. Old women cradled lifelike baby dolls swaddled inside the folds of crocheted blankets, and trembled as they handed them over. Anna had seen it all. How they whispered their goodbyes, planting secret kisses on treasured plastic cheeks and stiff woollen curls before leaving. Some would stay too long, like this morning's client, stories spilling out onto the long, oak surgical table that was littered with doll flotsam and body parts. Chubby legs and dimpled porcelain arms, splayed out and distorted, looked like they had dropped off some contortionist suspended mid-air. A shelf at the back of the workshop housed dolls that had simply been abandoned, their unfortunate fate sealed as they transitioned from being treasured companions to spare parts. Others, resurrected from the dead, carefully cobbled together from Anna's mortuary detritus, were reanimated into little human lookalikes.

Anna knew her customers were searching for their childhood, and like a true alchemist she distilled something from nothing to bring back those hidden moments of memory. The fleeting vision of a mother leaning over the bed, holding her palm against a child's feverish forehead to chase away the bogeyman of the dark, or a myopic uncle peering over the edge of his spectacles, his fingers gripping a chubby cheek in a pincer hold.

Surgery began again. Placing some glue onto the back of another glass eye that had a greyer, steelier hue, she slotted it inside the gaping socket. She gazed at Betty's two eyes staring back at her and felt a strange joy in their glassy silence. Anna preferred the company of dolls – they asked no questions. Instead, they just waited patiently inside her workshop – eternal brides adorned with yellowed veils, seated next to ambulance drivers ready to tend to the wounded. The debris of doll accessories – a *Wunderkammer* of broken prams, miniature houses, wigs made from human hair, leather boots and knitted clothing all piled into trays was every-thing that could ever be needed for a doll's comfort.

In the far corner of a top shelf sat a homely doll wearing a faded gingham pinafore, white anklet socks and black party shoes. Her name was Lalka, and she watched Anna's every move. Lalka was a remnant from her own childhood, an ambassador from the world of things and a memory of the dead – a parting gift from Mutti. To the outside world she had always been known as Lali. Anna cherished her first doll the most, even though those that came after were all poetry and precision by comparison.

Anna set her client's broken doll aside, waiting for the glue to dry. An earless bunny lay on the operating table, next in line for repair. It smiled blandly. Thankfully, this would be a quick job. An ear could be perfectly replaced, reattached where there is nothing important underneath. Eyes, though, demanded time, as Fraulein Schilling from the Puppetarium had taught her all those years ago.

They were the essence of a doll, the all-seeing holders of secrets. And always the hardest part to mend.

She was about to pack up and head upstairs when she heard someone knocking at the door.

PART I

Di velt iz a groyse un s'iz zikh nito vu ahintsuton.
The world is huge and there's nowhere to turn.

Yiddish proverb

CHAPTER 1

BIRDUM

FRIDAY 23RD SEPTEMBER, 1938

It was a small town, if you could call it that, tucked away like a hidden blemish on the underside of the world. Anna walked along the veranda of the hotel, its white, wrought-iron frame shimmering against the red earth. Even though the sun had set, the heat still felt stifling. Keys jangling in her hand, she fiddled with the rusty lock until she heard a familiar click. Strange really, this ritual of safekeeping – as if any thief around here could make a quick getaway. The wooden door creaked as it opened, the handle glaring at her with forlorn brass screw eyes. The last of the stragglers had wandered off to bed. Time to tidy up. She stepped into the dimness of the bar, setting a beer bottle rolling across the room. It rammed up against a large cabinet, rattling a collection of world globes.

Tell-tale fingerprints on the cabinet glass showed that Anna was a frequent visitor to this ersatz museum. She slid open the panel and sent one of the globes spinning. The world became a blur, borders losing their definition. Countries chased each other clockwise around the tilted axis of a globe. With one finger she stopped them

abruptly, then on a whim sent them hurtling off in the other direction. Instead of Australia following the rest of the world, she changed
the rules and sent Paris, Rome and Berlin off in search of Birdum.

When she first arrived at the hotel, she was puzzled by these
orbs. Why would anyone who chose to live in a place so remote
hoard so many worlds? She soon learned this very town was the
reason the collection took pride of place in Tom O'Hara's pub. If
you looked very closely, right there in the centre of the large continent, you could make out the fine, black letters: B-I-R-D-U-M.
Latitude 16 degrees 13' 55" S, Longitude 133 degrees 12' 04" E.
Several years earlier the town had started to appear on world globes,
reaching diminutive international fame thanks to its position as the
final terminus for the North Australia Railway. Situated at the end
of the line, Birdum prodded its way like some blind feeler groping
into the heart of the land.

Heralded by a pair of wooden beams, Birdum station was hardly
the Munich Hauptbahnhof. The weekly steam train, known affec-
tionately as Leaping Lena, shunted travellers to and from the city
of Darwin – a gruelling 320 miles to the north. After it traversed
the 100-yard bridge at Birdum Creek, Leaping Lena announced
its arrival with a clamorous shriek that drowned out its rhythmic
groaning.

The locals would come out to peer at the train's dark shape
approaching along the rusty narrow-gauge tracks. Finally emerging
from the surrounding scrub, the locomotive, followed by two
obedient carriages on enormous wheels, rattled along the rails,
coming to rest on a turning triangle beside a dusty platform. It
billowed black smoke into the air before winding down with
a loud wheeze. Limping dogs that lounged under the shade of a
veranda, occasionally snapping at flies, were always the first to hear

the train approaching in the distance. Everyone stopped what they were doing, or rather, took a break from doing not very much, and made their way over to the wooden platform where Leaping Lena prepared to disgorge her passengers. A lonely timetable was tacked to the side of a rickety railway hut:

Depart Darwin 8 a.m. on Wednesdays
Arrive at Pine Creek 4.46 p.m.
Depart Pine Creek 8 a.m. on Thursdays
Arrive at Katherine 11 a.m. on Fridays
Depart Katherine noon Fridays
Arrive at Birdum 5.51 p.m. Fridays

Earlier that evening Anna had sauntered across to join Leaping Lena's welcoming committee. The dogs whipped into a frenzy, except for Gubbins, who grimaced like a cranky old man. From the moment Anna had arrived in Birdum Gubbins started following her around, grateful for the scraps of bread and greasy victuals she threw his way. He would drag himself out from under the table, his unclipped claws scraping across the wooden floor, and hold out his paw like a tired beggar. His ribs were fine and delicate beneath mottled patches of fur. Staring at her, he would cock his head expectantly until she threw him a bone. There must be no better way to see the hidden secrets of a town in the outback, she thought, than through the eyes of a dog.

People usually spilled out from Leaping Lena and stood there speechless, surrounded by a few stunted trees drowning in a sea of tall grass, beneath the dome of twilight sky. Sticky from oppressive heat and humidity, the dishevelled passengers slumped their suitcases on the platform. The train was soon unloaded by workers who stacked up its cargo on the rickety platform. It didn't take long for the railwaymen, driver and passengers to walk past the row of huts scattered along either side of a lonely dirt road. They all ended up in one place – the Birdum Hotel, which stayed open late on train days.

The hotel was the most imposing building in town. Beyond its broad veranda it was a typical pub, with a few tables and chairs scattered around the entrance and rusty barstools hugging the counter. Several snake skins decorated the door frame. An old upright piano was huddled in a dark corner, its broken keys yellowed like an old man's teeth. A dried-out stuffed crocodile was splayed out along one wall, with its open jaws poised above a dusty patron who was focused on his tenth beer for the day.

The publican from the town of Katherine, Tom O'Hara, a tallish man with a tense face, had built the hotel in 1929 soon after construction of the North Australia Railway staggered to an unceremonious halt in the middle of the continent. The pub opened its doors during the dry of the following year. Birdum soon became a hub where people came from hundreds of miles around to get supplies. The O'Hara house stood apart from all the others in Birdum. Growing up, Tom O'Hara had been the most eligible bachelor back in Katherine, with a string of women across the Northern Territory left broken-hearted. During a drunken Saturday-night poker game, Tom won the land on which he would go on to build the Birdum pub. Not long after, he met Mary, the daughter of a textile merchant from Sydney. Four years and three daughters later, his wife and children – along with trunks full of matching handbags and shoes, department-store clothes and fancy toys – took up residence in the town, in a timber house newly built for their needs.

Anna had seen Tom O'Hara's advertisement in the newspaper soon after arriving in Australia, towards the end of 1933. The job included helping around the house, getting the girls dressed and fed in the mornings and then working in the pub each afternoon until close. He replied to her letter immediately, wiring money to travel to Birdum as soon as possible.

Three years after Anna's arrival, Mary became ill and took to her bed. Rumours spread that the family was cursed, and none of the locals dared to come near. The doctor had been sent for but it would take at least a week for him to arrive. Piled up on a table beside the sofa where Mary lay was an array of bottles, poultices and wads of gauze. A commode stood sentinel in the corner of the living room. Her dying was happening centre stage, surrounded by the audience of her young daughters. The oldest girl, Lisa, was only seven at the time. The child's eyes showed she was struggling to make sense of all that was happening around her – a mother who was meant to be immortal, now fading away.

Anna filled a heavy iron kettle and placed it on the stove. She cut the stale crusts off a ham sandwich, waiting for the water to boil. Arranging a cup and saucer and the sandwich on a tray, she carried it over to the sofa, being careful not to spill the hot tea. Mary had been so kind to her, teaching her how to run a house-hold, and introducing her to life in the outback. She showed respect for the local Yangman women, encouraging Anna to learn as much as she could about their customs and traditions, which was far more than most were willing to do in these parts. Helping Mary sit up, she propped a cushion behind her back. The woman took a small bite of her lunch, gripping a scrunched-up handker-chief in the palm of her hand, her knuckles shining white. Her jaw sagged open, the soggy bread falling out over her bottom lip and onto the blanket. She threw her head back and stared up at the ceiling. A soft, long moan filled the room, a tear trickling down her cheek from the corner of one eye. Anna steadied the tray.

'Oh, dear God,' Mary whispered, the half-macerated chunks of food falling onto the floor. 'What will become of my daughters?'

Anna knelt and held her hand. The girls were spread out on the rug in the middle of the room, Lisa hosting a tea party for her dolls.

'How am I to leave my children behind in a motherless world?'

Her tears turned to violent sobs, hands trembling as her breathing became staggered. The springs of the couch groaned with her restless agony. The teacup rattled in its saucer as Anna whisked the tray away. She turned to Lisa.

'Quick! Run and fetch your father.'

The young girl stared back, her childhood instantly stolen from her eyes. Grabbing her doll, she bolted out the door.

Anna felt the moment suddenly peel away; she was back in a darkened bedroom, lying beside her own mother, playing with the tassels of a shawl that covered the dying woman's shoulders. She nestled up close to her like a fledgling too young to fly. What lurked inside her mother's body, devouring all her beauty and sparkle? Skin, once so soft and smooth, now clung to bone.

She remembered birds chirping outside the window, greeting the new day. The sun filtered its way into the room, reaching out across the rug. Tulips wilted in the vase on the nightstand. Anna lifted Lalka from under the covers and placed her doll's lips against the back of her mother's hand. On the Friday before, they had visited the Tietz Department Store together in Bahnhofvorplatz, where Anna had interviewed every doll in the toy section before finally choosing her favourite.

'What shall we call her?' Anna asked.

'How about Lalka?' her mother whispered. 'That can be our special name for her.'

'You mean like a secret name?'

'Exactly, our secret. And you can choose a different name for her that everyone else will know her by.'

Anna thought for a moment, patting the doll's head. 'Her nickname will be Lali, but to us she will always be Lalka.'

When they got home, Mutti collapsed in the kitchen. Papa called for the doctor to come urgently.

Anna lay in her mother's bed, burrowing into the warmth of her arms. She breathed in the familiar scent of the cashmere shawl.

'I'll tell you a story,' Anna whispered.

It had always been the other way around, her mother recounting tales of trees the colour of rainbows with leaves of dreams, and deer with golden antlers hiding deep inside the forest. Her stories were peopled by barefoot shoemakers, witches who had lost their wands and bakers' children who never ate bread. Now it was time for Anna to conjure up some magic. She closed her eyes and tried to imagine something that would make her mother smile.

'Remember the lullaby you used to sing me when I was little?'

Her mother's breathing was shallow.

'About the birds who flew south at the start of winter, leaving their poor tree all alone. A little girl felt sorry for the tree and decided she would become a bird so she could go and keep it company. But as she was flying out the door, her mother told her to wear a scarf because it was so cold outside. Then she put a hat on her daughter's feathery head and finally threw a coat over her wings. The girl-bird

fell to the ground and the mother broke down in tears, asking her
never to leave her again.'

Anna held her mother's cold hand. Mutti spoke softly between
quivering breaths. Words escaped from her dry lips; utterings so
thin and floaty it was hard to make sense of what she was trying
to say.

'Shall I tell you more?' Anna whispered.

'Yes,' her mother whispered. 'I am listening.' Her voice had
become raspy.

'I'm afraid, Mutti.'

'I know.' She shifted slowly onto her side to face Anna. 'You will
be fine, my darling. I promise. Papa will look after you. Everyone
is waiting for me in Heaven – Oma, Opa, Tante Irma. They are
missing me, and I must go to visit them. But that doesn't mean I'm
leaving you, my sweet girl. Your beautiful new Lalka will always
be there to look out for you.' She gasped for air. 'And I will be
watching, snuggled into that little space behind her eyes, seeing
everything and everyone. If you ever need to talk to me, Lalka will
help you reach me.' She stroked Anna's cheek. 'Now let's both try
to rest a little, shall we?'

Anna turned onto her back and fell asleep listening to her
mother's harsh breathing. She woke at noon to find Mutti staring
at her, eyes unblinking. Sunlight crept in through the curtains onto
her mother's hair, which shone like flames.

After the funeral Anna looked around the bedroom at her
mother's things, none of which Papa, himself bereft, had touched
since her death – the sewing basket, an unfinished patchwork quilt,
the gramophone with a record still on it collecting dust. *Vergehen*,
passed away, people said. As if her mother had slipped out quietly
and was eternally sitting in her armchair, somewhere in the upper

storeys of sky, under the light of a reading lamp, crocheting the edges of a blanket, or mending the lace collar of her nightgown. A ghost who would never grow old. Anna felt her mother's presence. It had settled over the room, from the blotched ceiling to the bed on which they had spent their last hours together in this world, holding each other close.

In her dying Anna's mother unravelled like a skein of wool, tangled between day and night, life and death. A black-and-white photo taken three months earlier for Anna's seventh birthday showed them picking wildflowers together. They posed in the happy past, all colour about to seep out of their lives. Anna looked at the photo on the side table, the red buttons of her brown coat turned grey. Her mother's blouse embroidered with yellow daisies on a lavender background, now black and white. The camera's lens caught them smiling that morning, the memory like a rainbow washed away by a billowing grey sky.

In the days following Mary's death, Anna would hold young Lisa to her, feeling her warmth and quivering fear. They were both the inheritors of motherless futures. The child clutched a tiny doll Anna had made for her. It was fashioned from twigs and a wooden clothes peg, with a piece of hessian cut from a potato sack as a cloak. Although Anna dreamt in another language, there was never a need for fluency when it came to compassion. Terror swallowed words, but she could read this child's nightmares as if they were her own. She was well-trained in the art of being a lost child, no stranger to the empty foreboding that shattered entire nights. The memory of her mother's voice was like a soft breeze lingering in the leaves. The girl's face revealed the naked pain Anna knew only too well.

Mary was to be buried in Sydney, by the sea, far from the wind-beaten, cracked landscape of Birdum. The house juddered with Tom's grief. It was up to Anna to prepare the girls for the funeral, packing their cases with enough toys and clothing for their stay with their grandparents. Leaping Lena moaned and gasped as she carried them away, smothering the girls' sobs as they waved goodbye to Anna. Not long after, Tom decided that a widower like him would not make a good father – and that Birdum was no place for motherless children – so he sent them to live with his sister, their aunt Emmaline, in the Blue Mountains. Anna became manager of the pub and never saw the girls again.

CHAPTER 2

WARSAW

MARCH, 1938

Next door to the synagogue at 13 Tlumatzka Street, writers, actors and painters from across Warsaw gathered to talk, eat, laugh, smoke cigarettes, drink vodka, but most of all to argue. The Yiddish Writers Union shared the premises with Shayndel the Shayneh, who made a few zlotys on the side wearing knee-high black boots, a peaked leather cap and not much else.

Alter Mayseh was the secretary of the club and spent most evenings there. His nephew Yosl would accompany him on Wednesdays. The young boy looked after Shayndel's *tsedrayte* crazy white cat while she worked, wheeling the petulant animal around in an old pram. She paid Yosl with pieces of chocolate. It was also his job to pin up the Slave Market every week, a list of the various towns and villages where each writer was scheduled to give lectures on every subject imaginable, from Impressionism to the healing properties of garlic or the magic of gefilte fish. Yosl was small, so nobody noticed him as he sat drawing under the table, studying the sultry subterranean goings-on between the adults. He had a worm's-eye view of a famous poet rubbing the knee of a beautiful novelist, who in turn tickled the crotch of her husband, the editor of the gossip column in the local Yiddish newspaper.

'Yosl?' his uncle called. The boy sat very still in his hiding place and would have avoided discovery if Shayndel the Shayneh hadn't finished early with a client that evening and entered the room unexpectedly.

'*Ketsele*!' she called loudly. 'Here puss, puss, puss.'

The cat jumped out of the pram, mewing loudly.

Alter Mayseh pounced. He reached under the tablecloth, grabbed Yosl's ankle and dragged him out.

'*Ribono shel oylem*! God in Heaven! What are you doing there?'

Yosl was a scrawny boy, with spindly legs and a sunken chest, but what he lacked in physical strength he made up for with intelligence and wit. As articulate as he was, though, he answered his uncle with a lengthy silence. He held up half an apple, the juice trickling down his wrist. In the other hand was a crumpled-up piece of paper that Alter Mayseh snatched from him, smoothing it out to see what the boy had been up to. The sketch was ostensibly of the inner workings of the piece of fruit he was eating. But the child had been doing life drawing from his worm's-eye view – the seeds and folds resembling what Yosl had seen up the women's skirts, as the men furtively fingered them under the table.

'Get out, now, you little *zhulik*!' He pointed to the door, trying to hide his smile. 'You wild boy! Go straight home to your mother.'

Alter installed himself back at the table between Rinek, the new director of the Yiddish Writers Union, and a young man who sat hunched over, poking at a greasy piece of herring on his plate before slipping it between his lips. Yosl scooted out, leaving his uncle to talk to his friends about the problems of the world.

'Send me somewhere,' Alter begged Rinek. He tore a piece of rye bread in two.

'Believe me, we'd like to, but to be honest, there is really nowhere left that you haven't been, Alter – England, Denmark, Hong Kong.' He cleared his throat several times and coughed into his fist.

Although he had passion and talent enough for ten men, as well as drive, energy and a vision for the future in which he felt certain all people would live in harmony, there was one thing Alter lacked: money. He dreamt of travelling to a land of opportunity, where he could live a free and prosperous life.

'A young man surely needs a little adventure,' Joshua Singer chimed in. Alter wasn't sure if he was referring to him, or to Yosl's recent peregrinations under the table into the secret world beneath women's skirts. He thought he saw a smirk on the man's face, but it may have just been a *shmeer* of oil left over from the herring.

'I couldn't agree more. Thank you.' Alter smiled at the sycophantic freeloader.

'Enough, Alter! We have no money,' said Rinek. 'There is no *gelt* left to throw away on any more of your *luftgesheft*. All your outlandish schemes are founded on air.'

Rinek was a man with rheumy eyes and yellow teeth – a very average essayist, lacking in both courage and imagination. But Alter had to admit to himself that what he said was true. As the group's secretary, Alter had spent the past two years travelling between cities, villages and towns across Europe, selling subscriptions for the Yiddish newspaper. People invited him into their homes. Everywhere he went he was offered a slice of honey cake and a glass of tea with two lumps of sugar, all washed down with fantastical stories of scheming thieves, naïve princesses and demonic ghosts.

He witnessed firsthand the daily hardship in the *shtetls*: the cobbler's son walking barefoot, the tailor's daughter dressed in rags, orphans on the street begging for food.

'I haven't been to Australia,' Alter said.

'Why would you want to go to Austria right now, with all that's going on there? That fellow Hitler – a *cholera oyf im*, may he catch the plague – will soon gobble them up too. Mark my words,' Rinek snorted, a glob of snot catapulting from his nostril onto the white tablecloth.

'Not Austria, Rinek. Aust*ralia*.'

'Ah. *Azoi*! So now it's *ek velt* you want to reach – the ends of the earth! You, of course, would be the one asking us to send you there.' He slapped his thigh. 'Tell me something, Alter. Are you planning on becoming a comedian? Because you'd be very good at it. Maybe you should do that instead of scribbling *narishkeyten* for a living? Writing gibberish and nonsense doesn't pay the rent.' Rinek wheezed heavily as he tried to stifle his laughter. 'And, by the way, I'm interested to know: how does one reach this new *goldene medine* – isn't America your golden country?'

Shepsl Wolfe, who had been sitting in an armchair in the corner, his eyes closed, piped up: 'You travel to the edge of the world, then turn left.' An ardent overwriter himself, Wolfe had always been jealous of the ease with which Alter seemed to have poems accepted for publication.

'We know you are a *luftmensch*, my friend,' Rinek added, 'Always walking around with your head in the clouds, making up rhymes. But this is beyond all your wildest imaginings. Have you gone totally *meshuge*? It's sheer craziness.'

Alter pushed his chair back and stood up. He tugged at Rinek's sleeve, forcing the man to follow him like a puppy dog into the anteroom, where the Yiddish Writers Union office was crammed into one corner. They huddled over an old map of the world, which rested on a small desk. Rinek started to cough and splutter. Alter reached into his pocket, pulling out a handkerchief. He used it to wipe his friend's spittle off North America.

'Here,' he handed Rinek a small flask. 'Drink some of this. It eases catarrh.'

Joshua Singer had followed them and stood peering over Alter's right shoulder. His older brother Isaac, who had left for America three years earlier, was the former editor of *Literarishe Bleter*. Isaac had brought the lazy little *pisher* to Warsaw to work as a proof-reader for the magazine. He grabbed the flask from Alter and took a swig himself.

The outline of Australia was clearly visible, but someone had stuck a street map of Warsaw on top of it, making it difficult to prise the giant continent out from underneath.

'You see, Alter. That's a sign,' said Rinek. 'It's impossible to get to Australia, even on paper. And besides, what will you do once you arrive? Surely there aren't many Jews living there.'

Picking at the glue with his nail, Alter carefully dissected away the map of Warsaw. 'Allow me to give you a small geography lesson, Rinek.' He drew an invisible line around the great southern continent. 'Look closely. Can you see how Australia resembles a human head looking up at the rest of the world?'

Rinek grunted.

Alter took out his ruler and measured the girth of the country, which looked quite small on the Mercator map. He picked up a pair of scissors. Rinek watched him as he traced the outline of Germany and cut it out, fitting it inside Australia like a piece of puzzle. It was tiny by comparison. He snipped around Poland, followed by France, Belgium, Switzerland, and the UK, placing them all beside Germany. But even the whole of Europe couldn't fill the space inside the giant southern continent's borders. Surely, there was a tiny patch of land in this vast country that would take in a tortured Jew or two. After the Kishinev pogrom at the turn of the century, countries such as Uganda, Argentina and Ecuador had been floated as places of potential refuge for persecuted Jews, but it had all amounted to nothing. The British had closed off Palestine, so any vision he might have flirted with of longing for Jerusalem was unlikely to ever come to fruition. But that didn't bother Alter. All that mattered was to get as far away as possible from Europe before things got even worse there for Jews. He felt it coming, knew he needed to find a way to leave. How was he going to convince Rinek to approve of his outlandish new scheme? Perhaps he would start by simply telling him the truth and see where that led.

'Rinek,' he said, trying to sound somewhat dramatic. 'You know, I had such a bad dream last night. I woke up in a cold sweat. The village in which my family lived was ablaze and I was running from the flames with my brothers and sisters. One by one they fell, until I was the only one left.'

'Ach! You and your crazy nightmares, Alter. *Loz mikh geyn.* Leave me alone with your nonsense.' The podgy man, his sweaty brow furrowed, settled into a chair and opened a ledger filled with columns of spidery numbers. Alter knew this would be his response. Rinek wasn't one to believe in dreams. This lack of imagination was probably what made him such a lousy writer. Alter wanted to think that human beings could live in harmony within a global utopia. Now was the perfect time to realise his vision. Over the last couple of years travelling around from pitiful village to village in Eastern Europe, he had felt the urgency to find somewhere in the world that would take in a few Jewish refugees like himself. There he could build a community of like-minded souls, be the headmaster of a Yiddish school, grow his own food, set up a theatre troupe that would take the dramatised works of Bialik and Spinoza from town to town. Here in Europe, his people were increasingly either being shunned or subjected to violent attacks, no longer welcome in places they had lived in for up to ten generations. Most countries had immigration quotas akin to seven locks protecting their doors. Perhaps Australia, with its vast, gaping expanse, would only have six locks? It was worth a try.

He pictured himself in the far-off island surrounded by vast seas, a country that held a true promise of freedom. He closed his eyes and stabbed the map with a pin, landing somewhere north of the centre. He had to squint to read the name of the town he had landed on. Birdum. It had an earthy sound about it. He was a poet, after all, and must follow his heart, wherever it might lead.

Rinek interrupted Alter's musings. 'You know the story of the poor man who complained to the rabbi that his house was too small for his family of thirteen children, four grandparents and five cousins?'

Rinek was such a bore. Of course, Alter knew the story – how the rabbi told the poor Jew to bring his chickens inside, followed by all his goats and sheep. Finally, his cow moved in with the family. The very next morning, the man begged the rabbi to help him. The house had become so crowded and noisy it was impossible to live in. So, the rabbi told him to return all the animals to the barn. The man did what he was asked and when he came back inside, he looked around. 'It's so quiet and peaceful in here now.' He embraced his wife ecstatically. 'Look how much room we have, Rivka!'

Every story that Rinek told was burdened with a heavy lacing of morality.

'You see, Alter, you must never say things are bad,' Rinek said, lowering his voice to a whisper. 'Because they can always get so much worse. *Tfoo, tfoo, tfoo.*' He spat three times on the floor to ward off the evil eye. 'It's important to appreciate what you have. We cannot know what waits for us around the corner.'

Whatever might have been left of Alter's naïve vision of a global utopia was destroyed the following night, right on cue. His brother's grocery shop was looted and set on fire, windows smashed, swastikas daubed across the entrance.

He rushed back to the office of the Yiddish Writers Union the next morning and burst in on a meeting.

'Rinek!'

'Can't it wait, Alter? I have some important business to discuss with Joshua about Isaac's new manuscript.'

Alter had read some of the older Singer's hopeful scribblings. Even though the man was still chief editor of their journal, he honestly could have done with a thick red pen through many of his own clumsy sentences.

Before he left Europe he had attended one of Alter's lectures. Afterwards, he offered up a half-smile. 'You are quite the dreamer, aren't you? It takes a brave man to believe the world of justice will come today or tomorrow, where we all become brothers. And, sooner or later, no Jews, no gentiles, only a single, united mankind with the common goal of equality and progress. Ha! A *nekhtiker tog*! An impossibility, like the return of yesterday. I suppose you also believe great poetry will hasten us into this joyous epoch.'

'Yes, yes,' Alter said, trying to ignore the annoying *nudnik*.

There was always one in every crowd, droning on with their hefty dose of criticism just to garner attention. The man was a no-hoper.

Alter turned to Rinek, trying to hide his impatience. 'It won't take long. Please. I just had a wonderful idea.'

'You and your *narishkeyten*. All right, all right. Quickly then. *Nu?* What folly is it this time?'

'I figured out how I might be able to get myself to Australia.'

'Oh, really? Do tell us your incredible plan.'

'Well, I thought maybe I could canvas for donations there? I've found a fellow in a city called Melbourne who subscribes to our newspaper. His name is Retter.'

Rinek coughed up a plug of mucus, spitting it into his handkerchief. 'So, why not get this fellow to sponsor you?' He winked at Joshua.

For once, thought Alter, Rinek had come up with an idea that wasn't altogether useless. That same evening, he wrote a letter to their antipodean subscriber. A few weeks later, to everyone's utter astonishment – not least his own – money arrived for a ticket. Alter Mayseh – fundraiser and Yiddish poet – soon found himself on an old boat, bound for the ends of the earth.

CHAPTER 3

BIRDUM

SATURDAY 24TH SEPTEMBER, 1938

Refuelled and rested overnight, Leaping Lena started on the arduous journey back to Darwin at daybreak. A plume of black smoke billowed upwards in the distance as she made her way north again.

Tom O'Hara stood in the doorway of the hotel. 'Good morning!'

He interrupted Anna, who was lost gazing at the miniature worlds tucked away in their cabinet. She looked up at her boss.

'I need you to go check on the whereabouts of the mail truck today. It was supposed to get in from Alice Springs yesterday. I believe there's a passenger on board who was hoping to connect with the train. I guess whoever it is will be staying with us for the week.'

'Of course!' She wiped her dusty fingers on her apron. 'Right away.'

Tom stepped aside as she hurried past.

'There's no rush, Anna. It's Saturday. And they won't be going anywhere now until the train gets back in next Friday.'

The mail truck usually arrived towards the end of each month, after an arduous cross-country trek all the way from Alice Springs. It delivered tons of canvas bags filled with His Majesty's Mail to remote outposts along the way. This would be its last run for the year, before the start of the wet season made the terrain impassable. Anna always felt a hint of excitement whenever she heard the truck's wheels crunch over the pebbly drive, even though she knew none of the letters or parcels would ever be for her.

She had already finished her first chore for the day – gathering eggs from the hens. She set the chooks free to scavenge for grubs. Groups of apostlebirds would dart among swarms of flies that buzzed around the rubbish heap, their rapid-fire squawking mingling with the chickens' shrieking, all bickering over scraps. She loved the way they bathed ecstatically in the dust, covering their grey bodies with dirt. Kites hovered overhead, singing vibrato as they waited for the misstep of some unlucky lizard or mouse, before swooping in for the kill.

Every day she waited for night to fall just so she could go back home in her dreams, but at dawn Anna always woke to eucalypts tapping insistently on the corrugated-iron roof. She opened her eyes to harsh sunlight flickering between the branches. There was no need for an alarm clock here, the birdsong doing a fine job of bringing her right back to Birdum. The birds were a strange chorus – nothing like the sounds she was used to growing up in Europe.

Routine kept her from feeling lonely – emptying the commode, washing her face in a basin of water, combing her hair and knotting it into a bun. She chose a dress to wear, one of three she owned, and tied a clean apron around her waist. Finally she slipped on her shoes, carefully polished the night before to wipe off the

perpetual dust. She could hardly believe the woman she saw in the
mirror – blonde lashes, tanned forearms and naked lips.

Gubbins was stretched out on the veranda, snapping at blowflies. As soon as he saw Anna, his tail started to thump furiously
on the wooden planks. He was an unusual dog; sandy-coloured,
with a large head and narrow shoulders. Whip smart, he could slide
into the narrowest of spaces, wiggling his body out from the gap
under the door of the beer cellar where he slept, a veritable canine
Houdini. The Yangman women told her he was part dingo, which
would explain why he howled pitifully into the darkness every
evening, joining the night chorus of his faraway kin in the wild.

The build-up to the wet season had started early, the humidity
already stifling by late morning. There were only ever two seasons
here – wet and dry. Some of the men lounged outside under a
wooden awning, scratching their groins and slapping at mosquitoes,
talking about how early it seemed the rains would be arriving.
Those known as barflies paced up and down, waiting for the pub
to open. Beer o'clock began at noon and ended at closing. Punters
would line up in front of Anna, who stood behind the counter –
a priestess dispensing the holy sacrament of cold ale. The Birdum
Hotel was the watering hole for locals, as well as those who were just
passing through. Most of the regulars worked on the surrounding
cattle stations, huge tracts of cleared land at Elsey and Newcastle
Waters. They hid the harshness of their lives behind a veil of smoke
and alcohol. It was an easy camaraderie, which every so often blew
up into fisticuffs when a few too many beers had been downed.
Tempers could flare in the sweltering humidity yet conversation
was slow, silence more often than not taking the place of words.

With each year that passed, Anna found herself needing less
and less. How hurriedly she had packed her leather suitcase when

she left Europe, filling it with what she once thought essential. Out here it all seemed quite ludicrous – the heels, the silk blouse, the tapered woollen skirt. She had bundled up her belongings and left hurriedly. Now, the folded cardigan and stockings were tucked away in a neat pile on the shelf.

She moved about like a ghost, although she felt more spy than spectre, observing the customers as they sat at the counter waiting to be served. Silently, she watched mouths open and close, clam lips swallowing unintelligible words. And when the hotel's patrons got drunk, it sounded as though their tongues were falling out of their mouths when they spoke. Their craggy faces displayed a vastly different landscape from the European intensity she understood so well. Even a yawn was strange here – gaping and luxurious, instead of furtive and doomed to wither. These men embraced each gesture – their coughing, wind, laughter – unashamed of the orchestra of their bodies. And at dinner they took their time, chewing each morsel slowly, like actors in a play whose only role was to eat, swallow and belch. You could be fooled into thinking they were calm but, standing off to one side, Anna saw their uneasy fidgeting.

Fergus McTavish, the town's blacksmith, dressed in a pair of paint-spattered trousers, sat on the veranda leafing through the *Northern Standard*.

'G'day, love,' he mumbled, as Anna walked past.

Last wet season he had fallen into the river under the railroad bridge. He would have met his demise had it not been for one of the Yangman men hearing him mewl like a drowning kitten and pulling him out just in time.

Although it was a limpid morning, Anna's head felt shrouded in fog. Papa would have told her to 'take a walk to clear it', but that was impossible in Birdum – there was nowhere to go. A rusted

Castrol sign hung above the lone petrol pump that stood out the front of the hotel. A row of shacks lined the road, their windows decorated with faded curtains. She kicked at stones as she headed over to the town's water tank. Pat Dougan lay sprawled under his old truck, the pockmarked soles of his shoes peeking out. Gubbins mooched over and stood sentry beside him, scratching at fleas. Pat was a solid man. He wriggled from side to side and, as he bent one knee up, Anna caught a glimpse of his crotch. She tried to avoid imagining the bulge of stinking flesh tucked away there, but just at that moment he clamped his legs tightly together and loudly broke wind.

The town water tank at the entrance to Birdum had the best view in miles. It stored enough water to quench the thirst not only of Leaping Lena and her passengers, but of everyone who passed through the town. Anna began to climb to the top of the tank's rickety ladder to see if there was any sign of the mail truck. Reaching the top, she stopped for a moment to read a plaque she had never noticed before, embossed on one side:

WANDERSON & SONS
MAKERS
RICHMOND, VICTORIA

Such irony. A family with such a peripatetic name, probably ensconced in some comfortable city mansion while their work-manship braved the very centre of the outback. She looked down at the sea of lancewood scrub and spinifex grass encircling the town. Up close, scraggly trees with grey stringy bark haunted the fringes of Birdum. Others might feel the vastness of this flat vista strangling them like a noose, but Anna had grown to respect this landscape and relished the sense of freedom it offered. The wind whispered its secrets in her ear. She had arrived on a kind of reverse pilgrimage, not a striving towards anything but, rather, a hope of disappearing. To vanish, simply slip away from the rest of the world – that's what you could do here in Birdum.

She had been a quiet child. A girl who noticed the small things. Back then, she could never have foreseen that fate would take her to the other side of the world. As soon as she had set foot onboard the SS *Wuppertal*, she had been determined to submerge her past in the ocean's depths somewhere along the way. Crossing the equator, she had thrown her fur-lined winter boots overboard.

The bush held an abundance – the possibility of space, safety and promise. Kangaroos slept through the afternoon, under the shade of pale bushes. The light brought hope of change as the day moved from pinkish dawn to azure, jewel-studded evening. Night was alive with moving shadows singing mournful songs, an orchestra of strange voices, peppered with silence. Anna felt no fear. This unhurried presence, so distant from the rest of the world, brought her a sense of calm.

The horizon drew a circle around her. From the top of the tank, she had an unfettered view. To the north she could see a miniature city of giant ant hills standing tall. The mounds stretched as far as the eye could see, like an army of clay soldiers. To the east, the sky was bright, the land dotted with distant shimmering lakes, chimeras rising along the horizon. The dried-up riverbed was nothing more than a scar seeping into the red earth, lined with drooping scabrous trees that had given up all hope. In the distance, smoke from a small campfire prodded the sky. She looked down onto the small town below, people going about their business without noticing her. Some of the men were hauling steel railings towards

the station shed. Pat had strolled over to a bush and was unbutton-
ing his fly. From up there she could hear the loud tinkling echo as
he relieved himself.

She stood waiting atop the tank. This land, alternating between
desiccating heat and flash floods, demanded ferocious respect.
Any notion Anna might have held of it being exotic was replaced
by the reality of a harsh terrain, unforgiving to any stranger who
wandered off the main path. From up there, the hotel roof looked
like a giant Pinocchio hat that someone had accidentally dropped
from the sky. The building was arranged in a square, a tableau held
together by dirt and dust. A windmill raised water from somewhere deep underground. Lone, bleached skeletons of strange
animals lay strewn about, once connected by sinew and flesh. The
calligraphy of their tracks was etched into the sand. Splayed out,
this genealogy of bones looked ready to spring to life with each
setting of the sun, rising again in some ghostly articulation of their
former selves.

It had taken crossing huge oceans and vast tracts of land to purge
herself of all she'd left behind, but Anna felt safe here, protected
by the boundary of sky. It was a wrung-out shade of blue, faded by
the harsh sun. There hadn't been a drop of rain for 150 days.
Even the insects were too tired to hum this morning. As she gazed
out, the mail truck finally appeared in the south, at first a mere
crinkle in the horizon, surrounded by a halo of dust. A small part of
her wanted to leap off the water tank and hurl herself into the air like
a bird. She stood frozen to the spot, staring out at the vista before her.

Anna drifted back to childhood, to a secret hiding place in an
old pine. From her vantage point on a low-hanging branch, she
watched doves bathing in a crumbling stone fountain. A lone stork
passed overhead. Bees buzzed around a group of little wooden

boxes below, ferrying pollen from tall yellow flowers with leaves the size of ears. A black weathervane stood motionless, glistening on the roof of a grand old house. As a child she often used to daydream about how her life might unfold. Would she be like Cinderella, destined to meet a rescuing prince, or become one of the ugly sisters desperate enough to cut off her toes to marry? She preferred tales with happy endings over unspeakable deeds that crept stealthily into her dreams, littering them with giants, wolves and sneezing goats doomed for slaughter.

A voice called up to her, interrupting her reverie.

'*Allo! Allo!*'

She looked down. The mail truck was now parked below. A stranger stood beside it, staring up at her, his hand raised in a kind of salute to shield his eyes from the glare. His reddened face looked shocked by the sun.

'*Allo!* Lady! Must be nice view from there. This is what you do for fun around here?'

Even from up on the water tank, Anna could see his eyes flash blue. He wore a bow tie, sola topi hat and leather ankle boots. His high-waisted breeches were fastened with suspenders, a Box Brownie slung over his shoulder.

'I come join you,' he called, his voice reaching up, as if trying to hold her in a thin web woven from his breath.

He had a thick accent that sounded like some strange birdsong. She couldn't place it – Russian, Polish perhaps? He hung his hat on a solitary termite mound. Before she knew it, he had climbed up and was standing beside her.

'What are you doing up here?' he asked.

'It's my job,' she answered. 'I am from the Birdum Hotel, and we were waiting for you to arrive.'

'*Natürlich*.' Clearly recognising her accent, he switched to speaking German. 'Well, as you can see, I am here now. And only a day late.' The stranger removed his hat and bowed, then held out his hand. 'Alter Mayseh, at your service.'

'I believe you are headed onwards to Darwin?' she asked.

'Yes. That is correct.'

'Well, you've missed the train.' Anna started climbing back down the ladder without introducing herself. 'It left early this morning and won't be back for another week now.'

'So glad to encounter such a warm welcome.'

She bobbed her head back up, glaring at him for a moment. 'I am accustomed to greeting guests on ground level. I don't expect them to climb up here.'

'Of course. My apologies.' He stepped back from the edge and turned to follow her down.

Back on solid ground Anna extended her hand to the stranger. 'Anna Winter.'

He stared at her. 'What beautiful eyes you have – forest meets sky.' Alter Mayseh pulled out his camera. 'Come! Let us have a photo. It is fitting to commemorate this moment of our arrival after crossing the desert on this rusty steed.' He gathered his travel companions together – the stocky driver and a lanky Aboriginal youth – in front of the mail truck, and handed the camera to Anna. 'Would you mind?'

She stared through the viewfinder at the three disparate figures who stood stiffly beside each other, like puppets on a toy stage. She snapped the image that would capture the moment she met this curious man – a fractured piece of the whole.

CHAPTER 4

BIRDUM

SATURDAY 24ᵀᴴ SEPTEMBER, 1938

Max Schmidt was a pot-bellied, moonfaced man, with bulbous grey eyes that peered out from behind horn-rimmed spectacles. His thick German accent and a giant tiger tattoo on the inside of his left arm, alongside a keen ability to play *Ode to Joy* on the harmonica, added to both his crustiness and his gravitas. Despite standing at just 5 foot 1 inch, Max Schmidt was a force to be reckoned with. What he lacked in stature, he made up for seated behind the wheel of his 3-ton red Ford pick-up, which was an extension not only of his large personality but also of his general store. Travelling across rugged terrain for several days each month, he would stop at remote outposts to sell his wares of flour, sugar, tobacco, bridles, calico sacks and waterbags, all on credit. But anyone who forgot to pay him would be at the receiving end of a sharp reminder.

The man had always been one to keep to himself. No-one was sure where he had come from – like so many others, he'd simply appeared one day and stayed. You didn't ask questions in a town like Birdum. The windscreen of the red pick-up sported a large crack across the passenger side, a souvenir from an argument with Tom O'Hara four years earlier when Schmidt had decided to start brewing his own hops. In a town of so few inhabitants, that wasn't just stiff competition – it was an outright declaration of war. Not long after that, Tom O'Hara opened the fancy Lemon and Claret Room in the hotel, serving aperitifs and cocktails to attract more customers passing through town. This, in turn, didn't endear him much to Schmidt and the two became sworn enemies. They hadn't spoken to each other since.

Anna had barely said a word to Max Schmidt since arriving in Birdum, which felt strained at times, but Tom had sternly warned her not to have anything to do with the man. Despite their common language, Schmidt also seemed to avoid her as best he could, except for the occasional guttural expletive he would utter in German. His kelpie, Schmutzi, on the other hand, much cherished by its owner, was always looking for a pat and some scraps. She drew strange comfort from how it listened to her commands – *Sitz! Platz! Bleib!* – obedient in the way a German dog knew best. While heading back to the hotel with the stranger from the mail truck, Anna walked past Schmidt who was busy loading a pyramid of packages onto the back of his truck. Seeing Anna, Schmutzi raced over to greet her, wagging its tail in a frenzy. Gubbins, who had been trailing along behind, picked up his pace and launched himself at Schmutzi. They rolled around in the dirt, snapping at each other playfully. At least the dogs were friends, happy to share each other's fleas.

Max Schmidt was lifting a heavy wooden crate onto his truck. He stopped what he was doing and shouted, 'Schmutzi! *Herkommen!*'

The mutt obeyed instantly, cowering as it crawled back to its master, tail tucked firmly between its legs. Anna grabbed Gubbins by the scruff of his neck and led him up the stairs onto the veranda, ordering him to sit while she went inside to grab a bowl of water. When she looked up from the counter, Alter Mayseh was standing at the entrance. He seemed to be floating on the spot, silhouetted against a ray of sunshine. Pushing past him, she placed the bowl down in front of Gubbins, who waited for her command.

'Take!'

The curve-backed stranger watched the dog zealously lap up the water.

'I'm thirsty too.'

'The bar is closed.' She planted her hands firmly on her hips. It was too early for customers. Anna loved the time before opening. In between cleaning up and preparing meals, it was her precious time to be alone.

Alter Mayseh stepped inside and pointed to the clock on the wall. 'But it's just on twelve.'

'That stopped working years ago.'

He scratched the back of his neck and sat down on a stool. 'A broken clock tells the correct time twice a day.'

She retreated behind the bar and wiped a rag across the counter, tracing a wet line around his elbows. 'We serve lunch at noon. I'll show you to your room shortly.'

'I'd love a cup of tea meanwhile, if you'd be kind enough.' He smiled at her, looking rather comical in his bow tie.

'We are not in London, sir.'

He opened his mouth to speak, but she muted him with a piercing stare.

'If you wait an hour, I can pour you a drink.'

'You know, I think I may have found the answer to many of this country's problems. I've travelled all the way up from Adelaide to Alice Springs, then across the desert to here, stopping to camp at many places along the way.'

'Do tell.'

'Much could be solved by four words: more water, less beer.'

She tossed the rag into a bucket. 'I'll show you to your room now so you can get settled in before lunch.'

'Thank you. It will be good to sleep somewhere clean for a change. And, by the way, I'm vegetarian.' He grinned contritely.

'I have mashed potatoes.'

She led him down a corridor, stopping in front of a blue wooden door. Opening it, she motioned for him to enter, then turned around and strutted off back towards the bar. Alter dropped his bag on the floor. The hotel room reeked of dank, tired bodies, but it was far too humid outside to open the window. Sunshine saturated the sheer curtain – lace in the outback seemed so incongruous. He pulled out his notebook and flung it onto a rickety desk, then set out his razor, shaving cream, toothbrush, comb and pipe in a neat row on the washbasin. He always shlepped a Yiddish typewriter around with him on his travels, compelled to document his whole life in writing, afraid he might leave something out.

Even the walls seemed to be weeping over the dinginess of the room. He unwrapped a black crucifix from inside one of his shirts and hung it on a rusty nail above the bed. He had found it lying in the mud during one of his journeys through the Polish country-side several years earlier, jumping down from a moving horse and cart to retrieve it. Since then, he had carried it with him wherever he went. He couldn't explain why a Jew should feel such an affinity to a sacred Christian icon, but at the time there seemed to be some urgency in rescuing it and he had kept it close to him, hidden away, ever since. He lay down on the creaky bed, looking up at Jesus – or *Yoshkele*, as Alter's mother would call him, the endearing form of the Hebrew name for Jesus, *Yeshu* – staring down from the wall. He thought about how many men had become famous and respected only after their death. This was true not only for saviours but seemed especially prevalent among those with literary ambitions. For how long would Alter have to jump through a wall of painful rejections before his work found the level of respect he longed for? He didn't want to become that wretched type of man who only shone bright among the dead. Sure, Jesus was a Jew who eventually found popularity, but God knows he paid a hefty price for all his suffering. And let's face it, Alter mused, what was the use of eternal fame if your life on earth blossomed overnight, only to wilt by dawn?

A great believer in good health, Alter did his exercises religiously every morning. He filled a bowl with water from a bucket. Opening a physical fitness book that he had bought during one of his visits to Berlin, he turned to a photo of a man in long swimming trunks who resembled Bismarck with his bushy moustache. He studied the pose carefully, as if he had never seen it before, and contorted his limbs into a pretzel shape. After a minute or two of holding this position he doused himself with water, before proceeding to the next page. Ten minutes passed before he gave up. It was too hot to exert himself.

He glanced at the empty chair behind the desk. Lowering himself into it he stretched his legs out, spending what was left of the morning catching up on recording details of his recent adventures travelling north from Alice Springs – a trek littered with tiny cemeteries, stark reminders of broken hopes. His scribblings were interrupted by the smell coming from the kitchen, which made

his stomach rumble. He picked up his notebook and made his
way down the corridor to the dining room, which consisted of
a few wooden tables crammed together between the entrance
and the bar. That was where he found Anna, stacking up glasses in
the sink.

She looked up. 'You're back. I hope your room is satisfactory.'

'Any chance of that cup of tea now?'

'I suppose I can bring you one to keep you happy until the food
is ready.'

'That would be very kind of you. Thank you.' He paused
awkwardly for a moment and stared at her. 'You really do have such
beautiful eyes.'

Alter was sure he noticed the flash of a barely concealed smile
before Anna quickly disappeared into the kitchen. She returned
several minutes later with a tray. He sat at the bar, sipping tea while
he pushed his pen across the page. He stopped writing when she
came back to set the tables.

'Tell me, what on earth are you doing in a place like this?' he
ventured.

Several locals had begun to saunter in for lunch, sniggering as
they stole glances at the newcomer. Although, until now, they had
been speaking German, Anna abruptly switched to English.

'I live here.'

She slid Alter's open journal aside, setting some cutlery in front
of him.

Not at all fazed by the men, he stood and bowed to her.
'I didn't introduce myself properly this morning. My apologies. I am
known as Alter Mayseh, which means "old story" in Yiddish, but my
real name is Jacob Rosenzweig. My parents gave me the nickname
Alter, which means "old man", after their first child died, in a ploy

to confuse the Angel of Death. I am a Yiddish poet and writer from Warsaw, but first and foremost, I am a citizen of the world.'

So that explained his unusual accent. She lowered her voice as she switched back to German. 'Are you taking notes for a novel?'

'Diligently.'

'So, what have you written about me so far?'

'Ah. I am only up to the opening chapter. I will need to do a lot more research before I include you as a character. After all, I need to get my facts straight first.'

She tried hard not to giggle. 'Your letters are crooked,' she said, looking sideways at his foreign scrawl. 'But strung together they look like a chain of tiny flowers.'

'Well, I hope they are blossoms of truth then.'

She bit her lip. 'You have just enough time to write a poem about me before I bring you lunch.'

'But I hardly know you. It will be more fable than truth.'

'That suits me fine.'

She left him scribbling in his notebook and disappeared into the kitchen, returning after a while with several plates of sausages and potatoes, which she distributed among the men. Some had started singing loudly – most had already been drinking since morning from their private stashes. A long afternoon lay ahead of her. Anna placed Alter's lunch on the counter and sat down on a stool beside him. Pat let out a wolf whistle, which started a chorus of howls from the others, who had all turned to stare at them. This didn't seem to worry Alter. He tucked into his food like a hungry bear.

'Where's my poem?' she teased, ignoring the men.

'A man needs to eat first.' He shovelled a mound of potatoes into his mouth, barely swallowing before he continued. 'Besides, if it's a poem you want from me, then you'll need to show me some rivers that run deep.'

'They're all stitched underground here.'

He wiped his mouth with the serviette, leaving the sausages untouched.

'I'm vegetarian, remember?' he said, sliding the plate back to her.

Pat Dougan was sharing a table with Fergus McTavish. He got up slowly and strolled across to the bar. 'Who's yer new mate, Anna?' He picked up one of Alter's leftover sausages and took a bite. 'And why are you two speaking Kraut together?' He smashed his fist down on the counter sending a half-empty glass rolling, spilling rivulets of beer in its wake.

The men kept eating, seemingly unfazed by Pat's outburst.

'It's not a language we like to hear around these parts.' His speech was slurred. 'We don't want those fascist menaces invading. A country like ours is an invitation for them to come breed us out of house and home.'

Anna shot a glance at Alter and went to grab a rag to mop up the mess.

Pat turned to Alter, waving the half-eaten sausage in his face. 'You're a four-by-two, right?' He grinned, revealing three lonely teeth. 'Can tell by just lookin' at you blokes. Who else'd wear a bloody bow tie out here?'

Pat sat down beside him. Alter had heard the term before. Four-by-two. Rhyming slang for Jew. He'd been called worse. Kike. Zhyd. Sheeny. Smouch. Shyster. Shylock. Christ-killer. He was an instant curiosity wherever he went, a freak in some sideshow, even though he had no belief in God. What still made him a Jew, aside from his bris, a ritual he had no say in as an eight-day-old baby? For

Alter, it was language. Yiddish shaped his every thought, awake or asleep, wrapping its silken veil around his heart, coursing through his blood. Even if he wanted to, how to exorcise an angel that lived in every muscle and nerve in your being? A language filled with sadness, love, humour and wisdom, like none other he knew; and he could speak more languages than most. But it was a language without a home.

'Yes, I am a Jew,' Alter replied calmly.

'Well then, what are you doing around these parts? You lost, or something?'

'I'm looking for somewhere safe to stay.'

Pat quivered a little, then slapped him on the back. 'You know what? It's okay. You lot are a bit like white boys in my books. I'd be happy to carve out a small chunk of dirt for you to get on with whatever sort of witchcraft it is you do.' He snorted with laughter and turned to Tom O'Hara, who had just appeared at the door. 'Fancy that, boss. A four-by-two on our land. Would you ever believe it? Well, I guess a dog's gotta have its fleas to scratch, eh?'

Tom sauntered over to where Alter was sitting. 'Settle down now, Pat. No need to be rude. The man's a guest at this establishment. And a paying customer, too – which is more than I can say for you, lately.' He looked at his watch. 'Besides, it's only 12.30. I think you'd better pace yourself with the beers so early in the day, mate, or I'll be asking you to take a stroll outside to sober up. You hear me?'

Pat swiped angrily at a blowfly hovering around his swollen eyelids. He wandered back to his table and sat down, stinking of stale urine and beer. The man loved to pick a fight, although he seemed to know better than to try and start with Anna; after all, she was the one who ruled the beer tap. Only last night she had seen him arguing with Max Schmidt, and here he was looking for another outlet for his fear and loathing of foreigners. She detested him and his belief in his own noble nature, foolish oaf that he was. His face was a blush of anger, fuelled by alcohol, his eyes fixed on Alter with an intense disdain. Fate and time may have sliced Anna's life in two, but she certainly recognised bigotry and hatred when she saw it.

Tom turned to Alter and held out his hand. 'I'm Tom O'Hara, the owner of this hotel. My deepest apologies for my compatriot's behaviour.'

'Sadly, I'm used to it,' Alter replied. The man had a firm hand-shake, which usually left a good first impression. 'To be honest, though, I didn't expect it to follow me all the way here.'

'May I suggest you spend the afternoon in our cosy Lemon and Claret Room? You'll have a bit of peace and quiet in there, away from the local crowd,' Tom said. 'I built it as a bit of a retreat from the ordinariness of our little town.'

'Thank you. That's very kind of you.'

Alter gathered up his things and followed Tom down the hallway and into a side room decorated with tapestried rugs, velvet-covered armchairs and heavy brocade curtains. One wall boasted a row of shelves filled with books. A gramophone stood in the corner, beside a large collection of records. An upright piano took pride of place beneath a stained-glass window. The room was a dramatic contrast to the rest of the hotel, inside a town that barely existed. Alter picked up a copy of Dante's *Inferno* from the sideboard.

'My late wife loved to read.' Tom sat down, folding his arms across his chest. 'When I finished building this place, people came all the way from Alice Springs and Darwin just to see what was hailed as a true wonder. There was nothing like it for hundreds of miles. I used to run the Katherine pub, so I know the challenges that come with these sorts of establishments.'

He told Alter his vision had been to build a first-class hotel for Birdum, a repose along the way for when the train would eventually be able to pass through on its journey from Darwin down to Adelaide.

'One day this will become the longest transcontinental railway in the world. It will even outdo the Trans-Siberian Express. And when that happens, Birdum will be the central meeting place of the outback's road, rail and air.'

Alter admired and respected men who had absurd visions. Out here, under the constant eye of a defiant sun, this kind of feat would require a modicum of doggedness and pride, which the man seemed to have in abundance.

Alter smiled. 'It's already a very impressive place.' He cleared his throat. 'In fact, I received a very warm welcome from the young lady who works here.'

'Ah! Anna. Yes, she is a kind soul.'

'How did she come to be here in Birdum?'

'I brought her out here five years ago. Came to help with the wife and kids originally, but, well, after my wife passed, she stayed on to run the pub.'

'Do you know much about her family or background?'

'Nah. Keeps to herself mostly. Told me she grew up in Munich – but don't worry, she's a good egg, not one of those Nazi types. And she loves to read; that's how her English is so good, I reckon. Always has her head inside a book. She got along with my wife like a house on fire.' His fingers caressed the spines of a set of Shakespeare's works lined up on the shelf. 'You've come such a long way. Please. Make yourself comfortable and enjoy some rest after your difficult

journey. And I am so sorry you missed the train this morning, but
I do hope your week with us will be pleasant and restful.' He cleared
his throat. 'Again, I apologise for Pat's behaviour. He's not a bad
bloke; just can't hold his beer.'

'We say in Yiddish: *Khasene hobn zol er mit di malekh hamoves
tokhter*. He should marry the daughter of the Angel of Death.'
Alter sat down in a red velvet armchair. 'You are not to blame, but
I appreciate the gesture.'

Tom was about to leave the room when, as if by afterthought,
he asked Alter, 'What brings you all this way to Birdum, if I
may ask?'

'Of course, Mr O'Hara. It's simple. You see, I am a writer who
needs to understand where I am. I have travelled to hundreds of
tiny villages in Eastern Europe, and I know that you find the real
people of a country in its most remote places.'

'Well, we certainly fit the bill for Off the Beaten Track here, and
if by real you mean somewhat eccentric, then I guess you've found
that too. Anyway, I'm sure you are exhausted, so I'll leave you to
recuperate a little.' Tom looked like he needed a good sleep himself.
He stood rubbing his hands together. 'Right then!' He turned and
made his way back to the pub.

The Lemon and Claret Room boasted a library of dusty tomes.
Alter leafed through a collection of Australian books, settling in
to familiarise himself with the country's writers and poets. He
disliked detailed descriptions of landscape in literature, yet since
his arrival in Australia he found himself writing page upon page
about his surroundings, recording even the most subtle changes in
the land and sky. Yiddish writers busied themselves with character and narrative. The verdant, lush forests of Europe with their
meandering streams and deep rivers merely formed a backdrop to

collective memory. Jews mostly congregated in villages and towns, which formed the focus of place in Jewish literature. The musings of Australian writers he had read during his cross-country travels were languid and pastoral. In the glare of the sun, surrounded by vast stretches of flat, windswept scrub, an unusual calm descended upon him – deep stillness he had never felt before.

This country sometimes felt like a giant hallucination to Alter. In his travels across it, he had learned how the bush could be so moody, ready to cross you for the slightest mistake. One moment it embraced you, or at least allowed you to enjoy its beauty unfettered; the next it found all manner of terrifying ways to kill you. There were times aboard the mail truck that he had feared for his life – from a collision with a marauding mangy buffalo, to getting stuck in a bog that seemed to reach down to the depths of Hell. But death by landscape seemed a better alternative than falling victim to the wildfires of antisemitism and hatred rapidly spreading across Europe.

He picked up his pen, dipped it in ink and wrote in English, mouthing the words out loud as he wrote: *Nowhere have I felt as safe as in this wilderness.*

'It's not a wilderness.'

He jumped with surprise, spilling the ink across the page. Anna was standing behind him, looking over his shoulder. She threw the rag she had been holding onto his notebook and dabbed at the stain, ink smearing across her palm. His words lifted from the page and soaked into her skin. The sun peered in through the curtains. He watched her in the gilt-framed mirror, her hair shining like flames.

'I didn't notice you there.' He loosened his collar.

She smiled. 'Sometimes what's right in front of you goes unseen.'

CHAPTER 5

PORT PHILLIP BAY

JULY, 1938

Alter cradled the bird in his lap.

Vos zol ikh ton? What was he to do?

The majestic albatross had fallen from the sky and landed right in front of him, sprawled out on the deck, its broken wings spanning the length of two men.

After a lengthy crossing, having set off from Southampton with only ten passengers on board, the SS *Moreton Bay* was not far off the coast of Australia when the ship began to bellow and flail, grinding slowly to a halt. A flock of birds had been escorting them towards shore, covering over the sky like a swarm of bees hovering over a field of wildflowers. They screeched for scraps. Alter sat cross-legged, patting the injured albatross, who made no attempt to escape. One of the deck crew had told him these remarkable birds slept while flying – gliding and dreaming at the same time. They stayed aloft for months at a time without coming ashore, only to return to the same mate every year.

His first meeting with an Australian. Alter felt he had been poured into the bird, and if it were to sprout new feathers they would grow out through his own skin. The creature's breathing was rapid, the tiny heart beating wildly against its breast. The ocean, vast and ruffled with hope, stretched out before Alter. Behind them lay *tohubohu,* the chaos of a turbulent Europe. And here he was, having finally reached *ek velt,* the ends of the earth. It felt more like a new beginning.

He was in the thirtieth year of his life – perhaps around the same age as the bird, who the crewman also told him could live for up to six decades. He aimed to at least match that.

'You and me, we're both wanderers and survivors.' He stroked its back. 'But tell me, what will I do with you?'

The vessel remained anchored offshore, its engines silent, adding five unforeseen days to the biblical forty it had taken to make the crossing from Europe. Alter dedicated the time lost to caring for the wondrous creature, sneaking into the kitchen every morning to ask the sous-chef if he might spare a few scraps of fish guts for the bird. If it survived, surely it would be some sort of talisman, a sign that there was hope of freedom in this world for a few humble refugees? Each day the bird grew a little stronger, stretching out its broad wings in aborted attempts to fly.

Finally a tugboat arrived, carrying four crates of beer, two surly engineers and a customs officer on board. The engineers disappeared into the bowels of the engine room, while the crew busied themselves making inroads into the alcohol. Meanwhile the public servant, dressed in a suit and tie, clutched his clipboard to his chest and moved from passenger to passenger asking reams of questions and filling out lengthy forms. When he reached Alter, his sharp gaze already betrayed the intensity of his feeling.

'Name?

'Jacob Rosenzweig.'

'Date of birth?'

'27th of November 1908.'

'Place of birth?'

'Radymno, Poland.'

'Religion?' The man looked up from his paperwork, raising his eyebrows.

He was met with silence.

'Religion?' he repeated, sounding more irritated.

'I am of the world,' Alter answered. 'A non-believer. But very proud of my cultural heritage.'

'A Jewboy, then?' A smug grin crept across the customs officer's face. 'Anything to declare?'

Alter pointed to the albatross seated beside him on the deck and reached down to stroke its feathers. The official turned his back and moved on to the next passenger.

Just as they had all given up hope and became resigned to having to row into Port Phillip Bay in small dinghies, the engine started chortling, black smoke spewing from the ship's funnel. The engineers packed up their tools and climbed back down the ladder, returning to the tug, but the customs officer had disappeared. They all leaned over the edge to check he hadn't fallen overboard. Suddenly, a loud shriek pierced the air. Alter turned to see the albatross a few metres away from where he had left it. It let out an agonised cry, arched its back and crumpled in on itself, a trickle of black blood oozing onto the deck.

The rotund customs officer placed a pistol back in his pocket.

'Hey!' Alter ran towards him, yelling. 'Why did you do that?'

'Sorry. I can't understand what you're saying.' The man didn't look up, busily scribbling something into a notebook.

'Why would you kill an innocent bird?' Alter had to restrain his desire to throttle the officious little man.

'There are strict rules in our country,' he said, sneering. 'We do not allow vermin in, sir.'

He turned and walked briskly over to the ship's bosun, who helped ease the portly fellow back over the side of the boat. The official disappeared down the ladder. Alter looked across at the mess of feathers and blood sprawled out on the deck. He wanted to push the man into the swell, watch him being swallowed up by the waves, his body a delicious dinner for the sharks, scraps of brain served up as leftovers for the poor dead albatross's friends. The bosun nodded to one of the crew. The young fellow hauled the bird's corpse over to the railings and tossed it into the sea.

The *Moreton Bay* was soon on her way again. As they finally approached Station Pier, Alter Mayseh stared with disbelief at the meagre welcoming committee. Along the stretches of coastline on either side, in place of familiar birches, he saw the ghostly greys, muted greens and pastel blues of the southern continent he had dreamt of reaching for so long.

On his first morning in Melbourne, he sat in a café reading the newspaper. The Évian Conference, organised by President Roosevelt, had just taken place in France. Alter felt angry at the mockery of this outpouring of official concern, as the delegations of thirty-two countries paid lip-service by commiserating with the plight of German Jewish refugees, yet at the same time slammed their doors shut to any further immigration. The paper reported that Australia's delegate to the conference, T.W. White, claimed that 'under the circumstances, Australia cannot do more . . . As we have no real racial problem, we are not desirous of importing one.'

CHAPTER 6

BIRDUM

SATURDAY 24ᵀᴴ SEPTEMBER, 1938

Late Saturday afternoon brought with it a forlorn silence, searing heat rising from red hillocks that stretched out beneath the shell of sky. After spending a few quiet hours lounging in the Lemon and Claret Room, Alter Mayseh sat on the stoop of the veranda, a slim volume of poetry resting on his lap, its scrolled lettering defiantly exposing him as other. The company of these Australian men demanded compliance; he felt their stares. A twist of smoke rose in the distance. Shards of broken glass that had been trodden into the dirt in front of the hotel glistened in the light. He scraped his boot in the dust, carving out a crude smile. All around, the scrub whispered secrets, foliage drooping with exhaustion after months of relentless sun.

Alter's eyes were gradually adjusting to what had seemed, at first encounter, a monotonous landscape. Soon, tones began to reveal themselves. Muted drabness transformed into an ever-changing canvas of colour, daubed by the masterful brush of the sun. As it sank from this part of the world, it left behind its flaming outrage tattooed across the sky. Twilight faded and surrendered to gentle moonlight that dragged eerie shadows out from the tops of trees and rocks, drawing breath from the wind, unloosing songs from furtive insects that trilled in evening's cloak of darkness.

The distances some of the men had travelled just to find work were unimaginable. Days were long and sweltering and each of them seemed to live for that moment they staggered, exhausted, into the Birdum Hotel, polite as pie. The chatter rose, growing louder with each round. Anna was amazed a mere handful of men could create such a ruckus. A game of two-up got going on the veranda. By closing time the place looked like a crime scene, heated arguments often settled by a pair of fists. The previous night Anna had taped together a cracked lens on old Fergus McTavish's spectacles after he got into an argument with Pat Dougan, who had a reputation as a man who would pick a fight in an empty room.

'Your turn,' Fergus had said, egging Pat on to buy a round of drinks.

'You must have fallen out of an Ugly Tree and hit every branch on the way down,' Pat teased. 'You got a face like the north end of a south-bound camel.'

'Well, you're no oil painting yerself, mate,' Fergus replied. 'And yer so tight I reckon you wouldn't shout a round of drinks if a shark bit ya,' which landed Fergus a swift punch on the nose, breaking his glasses.

The damage Pat inflicted was of concern to everyone in Birdum. A blacksmith by trade, Fergus doubled up as the Overland Telegraph operator, as well as the official Puller of Aching Teeth. A loss of the man's eyesight would end up affecting them all.

A couple of drovers had been in town for a few days, on their way through to Newcastle Waters. Carrying its precious load

of benzine, their huge truck was beached over at the motor garage.
A knobbly bloke who had flown in from Daly Waters in his totter-
ing plane sat alone on an armchair in the Lemon and Claret Room
inside. His attention was focused on demolishing a plate of golden
fritters, an ersatz comfort after his rough landing on the newly built
airstrip. He had unstrapped his wooden leg, which lay abandoned
on the rug.

Anna prepared for the six o'clock swill, an hour-long intense
drinking session fuelled by the looming closing time.

'Last call!' she shouted, refilling the men's empty glasses as they
rushed to knock back as many beers as they could in the time left.

Tom had warned her from the very start she would be 'busier
than a butcher's blowfly' for that hour. But even though she had
been the only applicant for the job, and was young and inexpe-
rienced, she turned out to be the hardest worker he had ever
employed. As soon as the clock struck six, Anna ushered the
men out of the pub. They shuffled along sadly, like mourners at
a funeral. Lounging around on the veranda, they played another
round of two-up before each of them headed off in the direction of
their own rusty shack.

Anna locked the door and made her way through to the
kitchen. A kookaburra, perched in a nearby acacia, watched her as
she tossed some raw chicken guts into the backyard. The twittering
chorus had turned to silence earlier, and tiny bats darted around
feeding on insects. It didn't seem to bother the lone bird, which
had made up its mind to stay awake long past its bedtime waiting
for potential scraps. Its feathers flashed bright blue during the day,
but night had stitched a shawl of darkness over it. The bird cocked
its head as if to ask the same question every evening: *Can I trust this
creature who would feed a bird with a bird?* As the first stars appeared

it leapt down to unravel the sticky morsels. It pierced the meat with its razor-sharp beak and, holding tight to the prize, flew back up to the safety of the tree to devour its dinner.

That evening, after everyone had crawled home, Anna and Alter sat together on the veranda, watched by an audience of stars.

'Do you think it's as beautiful here as Europe?' he asked her.

'It has taken me time to warm to it.'

Memories and dreams floated beyond this absurdly wide horizon, rising again to haunt her. The glint of a glass, variegated patterns in a stone; the mundane and familiar evoked what was now so far away. A pot of daisies. A pink rose. Yellow daffodils awakening to spring. She often dreamt of home, the calls of the cuckoo and the starling. The land here seemed almost cruel by comparison, but it gave up its secret bounty for those who learned how to look.

She had been in Birdum for close to five years now. Within a day of her arrival she had already met all the people living in the small town, although hiding seemed a more accurate description for what most of them were doing there. They formed an unspoken pact, and this had become Anna's hiding place too. When anyone new passed through and asked about her accent, she mumbled that she was from Europe, busying herself with sweeping, or rushing away to wash the endless supply of empty beer glasses. She didn't lie. Not saying anything was the best way to avoid revealing the truth.

They were, overall, simple folk. The men could knock back beers without stopping, in a lingering version of suicide. When evenings started growing humid, the air inside the pub became oppressive and they took to sitting on the veranda, flicking their cigarette butts into the old horse trough. Their raucous laughter spilled out into the darkening sky. But at night, as she lay alone in her bed, Anna sometimes heard them wandering around outside, sobbing like children. There was a temptation for people out here to become greedy, lusting for what was not their own – the land's riches, another man's woman. But Anna knew from experience that it was those in the big cities, hiding behind elegant mahogany desks and their notion of 'civilisation', who made the most momentous decisions to embrace evil.

'It seems to me this is a place where one can have a new beginning,' Alter said, turning to look at Anna. 'Is that why you came all the way here?'

The cries of wild dogs hung in the night air; their calls had become a strange source of comfort for Anna in the depths of her loneliness. She prodded the wooden floorboards with a stick.

Alter persisted. 'Is all your family back in Germany?'

Screeching cicadas filled the silence.

She took time to answer. 'I belong to no-one.'

'So, what is it you are searching for here?'

'Only to live simply on this earth.'

'Well, at least you have that luxury.' He laughed.

'Do I? What makes you so sure of that?'

'Well, for starters you're not Jewish.'

She wanted to say there were other reasons to leave Europe, but shifted the conversation back to him. 'What exactly is it *you* are hoping to find here?'

'Me? I am just a Yiddish poet chasing a dream, looking for somewhere safe to rest his bones. How many more deserts and seas will my people need to cross before we can stop running? I could easily make this country my home – if only the people here would have me. The world is so vast. There's enough room for millions

more people, but the doors of most countries are closed – especially
to us Jews. We are living in a century that has its eyes shut tight. So
many hands, young and capable, are reaching out to seek work and
a new life, but nobody wants us. Sometimes I have a chilling vision
of what the future might hold. In it, I imagine the whole of Europe
rid of its Jews. A thousand years of settlement vanished in a thin
wisp of smoke. My very own language is filled with the hopeless,
downtrodden optimism that arises from generations of persecution.'

He took a tattered newspaper article out from between the
pages of his notebook and read aloud:

> *The Jews in every European nation are aghast at the horrors perpe-*
> *trated by the Hitlerites in Germany but are unable to interfere.*
> *The great scientist Einstein, who arrived from America on his way*
> *to Belgium, said he could not return home as conditions were too*
> *terrible. The outrages reported included that of Prof. Zondak,*
> *world-famous surgeon at Berlin Hospital, and his family having*
> *been beaten with sticks. At Frankfurt seven Jews were dragged to*
> *Nazi headquarters and there compelled at revolver point to flog*
> *one another until some were unconscious.*

'I found this in a pile of old newspapers on the shelf in
the Lemon and Claret Room. It's an article from back in 1933,
published in the *Northern Standard*. Do you know that in that
same year, over seventeen million of your countrymen voted for
the National Socialist Party? I wrote to Einstein about it. We are
both ardent fans of Spinoza. Even back then I told him the Jews
needed to leave Europe and find somewhere else to go. And then,
I had a strange dream about Australia. It's a land with so much
room for people in need of shelter – and so far from the hatred

growing in Europe.' He smiled as he unfolded another note hidden in his journal. 'See this? Einstein answered me himself, and even wrote me a letter of recommendation.'

Unlike Alter, never in her wildest imaginings had Anna planned to come to Australia – least of all this lonely, far-flung town with its corrugated-iron shacks and constant chorus of whirring insects. But the isolation here at the end of the line suited her.

She wanted to tell Alter this was also a continent of blood. If you dared to look, you would see it – an entire culture existing here long before Europeans, threatened too, their languages dying. She would watch the Yangman folk as they hid in the shadows on the edge of town, beautiful children staring out from behind their mothers' skirts.

'We live here without knowing the beginnings of this place,' she said. Without caring about its history, its past. So many of those who used to belong to this land are no longer, and we tell ourselves that what we bring is better. No need to look back or search for what was. And yet, at night, I hear echoes of their songs, their voices reaching out across time.'

'I have just travelled through the middle of this country for weeks. Do you think I haven't seen how badly they are treated, Anna, the pain in their eyes, their languages muted? It's all too familiar, I'm afraid. I was told there is no hatred in Australia, but I recognise persecution when I see it.'

The bush was quiet, the wild dogs no longer howling. Even Gubbins barely moved, waking occasionally to snap at flies, stand, do a half-turn and flop down again on the veranda. They heard boots tramping in the dirt as someone approached. A round face came into focus, blazing in the light of the lamp, a slovenly creature with a menacing stare. It was Max Schmidt. He muttered something under his breath, opening his mouth as if gasping for air. Alter stood to help him, but the man pushed him away, almost toppling over with the force of his anger.

The little man was all aflame with accusations, shouting in whispers, so no-one else would hear him. 'What are you doing, a woman of fine German blood, flapping around him like some silly bird?' He stabbed the air repeatedly, pointing to Alter.

Holding back for a moment, she surveyed the sturdy man. 'Do you have nothing better to do than make up ugly stories in your head?'

She immediately regretted the outburst. Even though there had been no more than a little flirtation between her and Alter, surely she could choose to spend her time with anyone she wanted. Schmidt embodied the very men she had travelled all this way to escape, yet here he was right in front of her, waving his Jew-hatred under her nose. And what made someone so obnoxious just because of their race, anyway? Did Schmidt think some bewitching entanglement had drawn her towards Alter, who was a flesh-and-blood human being like any other? The horrid man was calling her to account for something that, even if it were true, she would never be ashamed of. Schmidt stood before her demanding an answer, but the words she wished to form became choked with rage.

'Filthy swine,' Schmidt yelled. '*Jude!*' He spat at Alter, and hobbled away, vanishing into the darkness.

That night, neither moon nor stars appeared. Rain clouds rolled in, cloaking Birdum with the threat of its first downpour.

CHAPTER 7

MUNICH

FEBRUARY, 1933

Papa's leather suitcase was unremarkable, held together by a brass buckle at the end of a strap. It lay open on the bed. Anna looked down at her folded belongings: a cotton nightgown tucked between three frocks, an olive-green cardigan, a woollen skirt and her good silk blouse. Such scant cargo for a journey across vast oceans. She gazed up at the pale sky beyond the trees; the winter had been bleak, with no real sunlight since November. Maybe others saw silvery sunshine and soft falls of dusk, but for Anna the days slid from dimness into darkness and back again. Sometimes when she woke it was hard to tell whether it was morning or still night.

It would be hot where she was going. How to prepare for a climate she knew nothing about? A world so far away. But clothes were not her real concern. The most precious cargo was her collection of small costume dolls she couldn't bring herself to leave behind. She had fashioned a safe compartment for them, each one housed in a tiny roll of material, then tightly wrapped in underwear or socks. The Dutch doll proved the hardest to pack, the wings of her white hat poking holes through Anna's fine wool stockings. The wooden clogs kept falling off the doll's tiny feet, so Anna ended up gluing them on so they wouldn't get lost. She locked the suitcase and slid it back under her bed. The train would leave that day at 8 a.m. She whispered the instructions to herself like a kind of mantra.

She had walked five miles through the viscous grey chill of dawn, clutching her suitcase, to visit the man her papa called Shmontz. He was so small you could almost mistake him for a child, were it not for the feathery tuft on his chin – not the sort of person she imagined would work clandestinely for the Resistance. She had watched him as he examined the envelope of papers Papa had prepared. The man flicked aside a streak of blond hair that kept falling across his forehead. His left eye was black. It was rumoured that his vision had been destroyed because of constant exposure to chemicals as a young apprentice working in a clothes-dyeing shop. The damaged eye kept lolling disconcertingly outward, blindly staring down at the stacks of books that surrounded him. He held a magnifying glass up to his good eye as he examined the documents. Despite his youth, Shmontz already had a discreet reputation beyond the Jewish community as the master of erasure, disappearing real identities to carve out plausible new ones.

'Will you be able to help me vanish in time?' She clutched the bag to her chest, her foot tapping out a nervous rhythm.

The young man sized her up with a prickly gaze. 'Small fictions can't be rushed.' He placed the magnifying glass back down on the desk.

'If we don't move quickly, they will find me.' Anna was trying to be careful not to aggravate him. She knew her fate hung on every detail he inscribed onto one of the blank identity cards he pulled from a drawer.

The room was filled with junk, the flotsam and jetsam of his unknowable life. A naked mannequin stood behind him. It bore the anonymity Anna was desperately seeking. On the desk lay a pile of rubber stamps, inks of various colours, an old typewriter and a jar filled with pens. A grey-and-white cat sat on a cushion beside him, licking its paws.

'I am very grateful to you,' Anna added, handing over the money Papa had instructed her to give Shmontz. In return, he would provide her with the papers that would allow Anna Müller to cease to exist. It was a risk she had no choice but to take.

A faint smile came across his face as he focused on the documents. He placed them back in the envelope which he flicked into her palm, as though he were performing some magic trick.

'No problem,' he said. 'It's my job to change someone's life *in einem Augenblick.*'

In the blink of an eye, she had become Anna Winter.

CHAPTER 8

BIRDUM

SUNDAY 25TH SEPTEMBER, 1938

On Sunday she had free time to do as she pleased. Yet there was something in the spaciousness of a day off that made Anna feel like she was submerged in a vat of molasses. It was during those empty hours that the endless dead pursued her, even in this far-flung landscape. Just when she began to think she had eluded the ghosts they would step out into the open, startling her with their presence. Sometimes, looking at herself in the mirror, she felt dizzy with longing as her mother's reflection emerged like an echo, pulsing with youth.

Today the dead seemed to have decided to leave her alone. She had promised to show the Yiddish poet around – but after a quick lap of the town, they ended up climbing back up the water tank, where they had met only a day earlier. The sky had turned grey that morning for the first time in months. All around them trees gripped the clouds, refusing to release them back to the sky, but the ruthless wind blew up and snatched them away again.

'Tonight is *erev Rosh Hashone*, the eve of Jewish New Year, when we celebrate the creation of the world. But it's also a Day of Judgement. The wicked are condemned to eternal damnation, while those who have been good are granted yet another year to roam the earth.' He turned and smiled at her, to lighten the mood.

'Jews like me,' he went on, 'who sit on the fence about both religion and the existence of God, are given another chance to repent for our sins over the next ten days – *Yamim Nora'im*, the Days of Awe. And then comes *Yom Kippur*, the Day of Atonement, when we fast and our fate is finally sealed in the Book of Life. That's the time for *Yizkor*, a prayer for remembrance, where we call out the names of our dead.'

'It's a nice custom to acknowledge the presence of those we've lost,' she reflected.

'You think so? To my mind it's ridiculous. Do you really think the dead are listening, or that anyone can see them?'

'I guess you need to know how to look,' she answered thoughtfully.

'So how long does it take for them to appear then?'

'They never disappear.'

'I, for one, would rather pay attention to people who are right here in front of me.'

He felt deprived he had no direct line to his grandparents, Bubbe Fruma or Zeyde Shepsl. They would probably be *broyges* with him by now, furious he hadn't made more of an effort to bring them back from the dead. How he would love them to visit him in this world. But what would they say if they saw him so far away from home, flirting with a woman of whom they would never have approved? The work of the eyes was overrated, he decided. He didn't need to see them to hear their voices in the air, tormenting him over this almost-transgression. He was breaking with tradition, the weight of guilt imposed on the living by the dead.

'*Oy vey!*' Bubbe Fruma would wail. '*A shikse* is not enough for him. No, no. This one has to go and find a German gentile woman as well, *nokh*. And on *erev Rosh Hashone* too, a high holy day. What a wonderful way for him to start a New Year, with a sin.'

'Why do you always have to get so hysterical, Fruma? He's only talking to the woman. He hasn't done anything wrong.' Zayde Shepsl interrupted her tirade.

'Not yet. *Aza shande*, it's such an embarrassment for the family. At least he has until *Yom Kippur* to atone.' She spat three times. '*Tfoo, tfoo, tfoo.* My own grandson is killing me.'

'He can't kill you, Fruma. We're dead, remember?' Zeyde Shepsl said.

'Akh, dead shmead. *Altsding lozt zikh oys mit a gevayn.*'

'No! Not everything has to end in tears, Frumaleh.' He put his arms around her as she cupped her face in her hands.

Alter always thought that ghosts were canny inventions to remind children not to entertain thoughts of going astray. His mother used to tell him that spirits of the dead possess the living, because they still have a reckoning to make with those they left behind. If that was true, he wondered why the chicken feet poking over the rim of the pot of soup didn't simply climb out and scratch his mother's face before they ran away. As a child, he thought he possessed magical skills to bring the dead back from wherever it was they went to hide. He embellished them with supernatural powers: the milkman's horse, who had died the week before, returned sporting two heads instead of one, each with an extra pair of eyes looking backwards. When he shared the stories he invented with his mother, she would forbid him from telling Father, who was a pious and brooding man.

No, there was good reason for a boundary to exist between the living and the dead. Alter knew it would be impossible to flourish in love under his dearly departed's watchful lingering, always so judgemental in their mistrust of mortal transgressions. He felt a sudden wave of nausea rising, his heart pounding. He closed his eyes and swayed a little. He thrust his arms forwards to clutch the edge of the tank before collapsing with a thud. He lay there in a crumpled heap. Anna had never seen anyone faint before. It wasn't as poetic as she had imagined. She propped his head up.

'Thank you. I'm fine,' he muttered, holding his hand on top of hers for a moment.

'Let's get you down from here.' She peered over the edge and saw Johnnie, one of the Yangman elders, a fine cattleman from Elsey Station, standing over to one side, smoking a cigarette.

She called down to him and within moments he had clambered up the ladder and helped Alter down, his arm around him as they hobbled back to the hotel.

'Come,' she said to Alter. 'You should put your feet up for a while. My room is closer.'

She led the poet inside, towards her fuggy little room, which was not much more than a nook behind the kitchen. A wooden bedside table stood beside the metal cot, pushed up against one wall. He lay down on the bed.

'Are you feeling any better?'

'Yes, thank you. I'll be fine. I don't know what came over me. I just felt very dizzy. Maybe the long journey is finally taking its toll.'

He looked up at a rickety shelf from which Anna's dolls stared down at him.

'You have a lot of toys.'

'Dolls,' she answered with a faintly mocking smile. 'They are my collection, not my toys.'

'Dolls, yes. Of course. They look like a little family.' He sat up. 'This bigger one at the end has the same eyes as you.' He reached up to take Lalka down from the shelf.

'Don't touch her!' she shouted. 'That's Lali. She's special,' she added quietly, embarrassed by her outburst.

'My apologies.' He lowered his arm. 'But if I may be honest, she's no beauty queen.'

'You don't need to be perfect to be loved.'

He folded his arms in front of him.

'You know, I was never allowed to play with toys as a child,' he said. 'My mother lined them up on a shelf, out of my reach, because she didn't want me to break them.'

'That's sad.'

'One day,' he continued, 'when mother had gone to the fish market, I climbed up and reached the *Do Not Touch* shelf. The tin soldier wobbled and teetered over the edge. Before I could catch it, it plummeted to the ground and lay there, its head twisted, body split open. I jumped back down and held it like a surgeon, keen to see its soul now that the toy's secret life was open to inspection. I still remember the melancholy seeping through me as I was robbed of the belief that the toy soldier had a life.'

The man was full of stories. She had her own that she longed to share, but she kept them to herself.

'Why do you collect dolls?' he asked.

'Because I love them. Dolls are a way to recapture the innocence of childhood. They hold our memories.'

A doll was a confidante, following its owner around, dragged from place to place like a loyal servant. From the first awakening soon after birth to the loneliness and abandonment felt in the crib, a doll accompanied the smallest of humans across feverish nights and terrifying dreams, patrolling the edges of childhood. Listening without hearing, falling to the floor without protest – all the while bearing witness. Their inert bodies were a receptacle for sadness and secrets.

'And dolls never die,' he said.

There was a pause in the conversation. Like a giant wave, frozen mid-air.

'Please tell me your story, Anna. I would very much like to get to know you.'

'There is no story. Nothing to tell.'

Her previous life coiled up inside her like a snake. Anna tried to make herself small in this place, going about her chores, cleaning the pub after the evening's indulgence, during which the men drowned all their sorrows in beer. Her story was hers alone and would remain a secret, hidden only inside memory, or midnight hauntings. She wanted to lose her old language in the new one. Until this stranger turned up, comical in his sola topi, bow tie and high-waisted trousers, her life had been divided into before and after. Just as she was ready to completely let go of the old world, he arrived along a dusty track, emerging from the scrub.

'Each of us has a story,' he said. 'Granted, some more interesting than others.'

'Indeed. But we are both small characters, inserting our own absurd tales into this land. I grew up in Germany. That part of my life is thankfully over. That's all there is. I am embarking on a new story.'

'You must have witnessed some pretty dreadful scenes there as a young girl. Is that what made you leave? Just because something has happened in the past doesn't mean it's over, especially in the part of the world we have come from. History has a habit of washing up like a tide onto the shores of the present. And we can choose to bathe in these waves, swim through them – or else risk drowning. But I do agree, we must look to the future – that is where I live.' Alter pointed to the horizon. 'Over there, where I have never been, is where I long to go.'

Beneath every secret lay shame. That is why a secret was kept in the first place. Anna tried to swallow her past, but it stuck in her throat – everything she had seen with a child's eye refused to disappear. She could walk through the rooms of their apartment in Munich, stand by her bedroom window again looking out onto the huge plane tree. In her mind's eye she could trace her way to her parents' room, padding along the rug in the hallway, and pull out the secret drawer in the armoire in which Mutti hid her personal trinkets – a silver thimble, a crochet hook and a tiny gold star on a chain. Memory had frozen everything in its place, unmoving, even the basket of unfinished knitting.

But there were times when a memory hit her like a lightning strike – a child stranded in grief, confused by the smoke and mirrors of the adults who surrounded her. She pictured young men marching through the streets wearing crisp, brown uniforms perfectly ironed by their doting mothers. Anna could not bury history, try as she might. It lived inside her, always slightly blurred and out of reach. And that space held so many questions, waiting for the clarity of some answer to appear.

'You can rest here for a while, Mr Mayseh,' she said.

'Please, call me Alter.'

'Of course, Alter. I'll go make some tea. If you need me, I'll just be next door in the kitchen.'

She boiled the kettle. Placing a cup and saucer and some biscuits onto a tray, she made her way back to her room. Alter was gone, the linen on her bed smoothed out. An ink-smudged note rested on her pillow. It was a poem, written in German:

I am a passing stranger
do not know the names
of all the chambers in your heart
your eyes dip like swallows
drinking from the tide of souls
invisible paths left behind through clouds
I try to read your secret map of grief
find my way one heartbeat at a time
an ancient tale lies hidden in those bones
ghosts watch over you through sleep
moon eyes darting wildly in your dreams
an injured bird to cradle in night's arms

She folded the piece of paper in half and hid it in a drawer, then sat on the edge of the bed and drank the tea herself. It was getting late. She did a round of the hotel to check the doors were locked and headed off to bed.

CHAPTER 9

LANDSBERG

SATURDAY 24ᵀᴴ MAY, 1924

Anna woke with a jolt as the car bumped down a laneway. She grabbed Lalka by one leg to stop her falling off the seat. Papa pulled up in front of an old shop. Professor Jäger, impatient to get out, opened the door himself, sending an icy wind piercing through her bones.

'Wait here, Gustav.'

Papa left the engine running. He sat behind the steering wheel, staring straight ahead, as though his head were fastened to the collar of his grey chauffeur's uniform. His hat had a tiny feather sewn into the felt braid.

Anna yawned. They had left Munich before dawn, and she had drifted in and out of sleep along the way.

'Hello, my princess.' He turned to face her. 'Are you hungry?'

'Not really, Papa.' Her tummy rumbled loudly, betraying the truth.

He handed her half a sandwich.

'We're almost there, darling. Are you excited?'

'Yes, Papa.'

He lit a cigarette and took a few quick puffs. In the long year since Mutti had died, this was the first time Anna had been invited to visit the professor's huge country house in Landsberg am Lech. Up until then Papa had driven to and fro over the weekend, while Anna spent hours alone in her room playing with her toys. But from now on she would be joining Papa each weekend in Landsberg. She was looking forward to this new adventure. She had filled her satchel with a notebook and pencil, a spare pair of socks and a carefully chosen doll to show Professor Jäger, whom Papa told her was a keen doll collector. And of course, Lalka came too.

The sun was trying to peek out from behind heavy clouds. Trees held onto their frosty buds, doubting that spring had arrived.

'Anna, darling,' Papa blew a smoke ring. 'I just want you to remember that sometimes things are not always what they seem.' Through the foggy window Anna watched Professor Jäger as he knocked on a blue door to which a wooden sign was nailed.

Pignataro's Puppetarium stood on a corner of the main street and a small alleyway. A family of wooden marionettes hung in the window display – a woman, a man and three children – all coated in a thick layer of dust. They looked terrified but had no mouths to scream. The only part of their faces that had been painted on were the eyes, which gave them a barely human appearance – a ghastly theatre of ghouls. Anna thought they might have been the kind of dolls used by an old witch. The light shining in cast long, thin silhouettes of the puppet family onto the side wall.

Huddled inside his thick overcoat, the fur collar turned up to warm his neck, the professor stood waiting as he hopped from one foot to the other. He rubbed his hands together, wisps of foggy breath curling upwards into the cold air. A short woman answered, her hair tucked under a red scarf. They exchanged a few words before she pulled out a small package from the pocket of her apron. Professor Jäger slipped the parcel inside his coat. Looking around for a moment, he hurried straight back to the car, motioning for Papa to leave.

They followed the river Lech as it wound its way through the centre of Landsberg, past the main square. The village, with its candy-coloured houses and cobblestone streets, looked like it had sprung from the pages of a book of fairytales. Under the shadow of a tall tower, market stalls were piled high with greens and fruit, sides of pork strung up beside giant sausages. Chickens and ducks huddled in wicker baskets. Anna's eyes feasted on the vibrant scene as they drove past. She could hear the muffled cacophony of people selling their wares, hoping dearly that the professor might ask Papa to stop the car. Instead he sat motionless, his gaze fixed upon the parcel now resting in his lap as the market disappeared behind them.

The car snaked along a winding road. On the outskirts of the village Papa turned left into a driveway, which led to a grand house guarded by gargoyles. The sun had crept higher in the sky, melting the layer of frost blanketed over the landscape. Between the trees Anna glimpsed the shimmering surface of the river at the bottom of the garden. An elderly gardener was busy tending to flowerbeds lush with lavender and cornflowers. He rested his rake against an old wheelbarrow and stood scratching his beard as he stared at the arrivals. This time Professor Jäger sat still as the car pulled up, waiting for Papa to run around and open the rear door for him. Anna slid across the leather seat and hopped out next, Papa winking as he patted her head. The gardener, smelling of dung and compost, doffed his cap as they walked past. Anna waved shyly and he raised his hand hesitantly in response, his fingernails blackened with dirt.

A tall butler stood inside the entrance. With his left arm extended he had turned himself into a living coat stand, staring at a point on the opposite wall, his twitching bushy eyebrows the only part of him that moved. Papa carried the bags inside and arranged them at the foot of the stairs. He straightened his jacket and whispered something to a young housekeeper, who wore a starched white apron tied around her waist. She curtsied, turned and hurried down the corridor. Professor Jäger threw his coat over the butler's arm and disappeared into a side room, closing the door behind him. Papa lugged the suitcase up the staircase, followed closely by Anna, who carried the bag that held her dolls. At the top of the landing he opened the door to the first room on the left. He flung open the curtains and Anna rushed to look out the window. Red geraniums cascaded down from an ornate wrought-iron window box. Below, a lone apple tree grew in the centre of a vegetable patch that was surrounded by low brown-brick walls. A huge garden gradually changed from manicured to wild as it sprawled towards the river's edge.

'This is where you will be staying, sweetheart.' He placed her suitcase at the end of the bed.

'And you, Papa?'

'I'll be downstairs in the servants' quarters if you need me. But don't worry, you'll be fine. Now leave your things here and go explore the grounds. I think you'll love the garden. The housekeeper will let you know when lunch is ready.'

Papa walked towards the landing. She heard his footsteps halt for a moment as he headed downstairs.

He called up to her: 'I'll see you later this afternoon, darling.'

Anna felt a little sorry for Professor Jäger. It was such a large place for a man to live in all alone. He seemed quite sad. Deciding she would explore the house later, Anna raced out to the garden, carrying Lalka in a small bag. Making her way across a meadow, she passed a flock of sheep who were too busy grazing to notice her. The mountains in the distance were still snow-capped, but the sun was warm now. Spring had arrived at last; lambs were wagging their tails, crickets whirred and ducklings darted around lilies on the pond, frantically trying to catch up to their mothers. A fringe of birch saplings grew along the bottom of the garden. Beyond them lurked the giants of the forest, oak and fir trees towering over glades of woodland ferns.

She followed a narrow path lined with daffodils and sat down under the shade of a giant oak, ringed by a carpet of moss. Peeling off her shoes and socks and slipping them into her satchel, she tiptoed down to the riverbank, mud squelching between her toes. A few iridescent blue beetles scuttled out of the way as she inched her way into the water. Small fish approached cautiously, some of the braver ones daring to nibble at her ankles. A mother ushered her ducklings across to a small island in the middle of the river, commanding them with a gentle but firm quack to hide among the reeds. Anna scrambled up an old willow tree that dipped its fronds into the water.

The forest felt alive with strange, whispering creatures. The *Waldgeister* would surely be nearby, skulking around his demon cave inside a large pine. And the *Holzfrau* too, protector of ancient trees, her tangled strands of moss hair dragging on the ground behind her as she limped along pushing a broken wheelbarrow. Reaching out to the gardener, she would ask for food and, if he was kind to her, she would reward him with a pile of woodchips, one of which would turn into gold at midnight. But if he refused, then her nails would instantly transform into sharpened claws and she would scratch a permanent reminder to be kind to strangers right across his face.

Elves watched Anna from their hiding place underground. They had left behind rings in the grass, a sign they had been dancing hand in hand under the moon the night before. As the children of witches and devils they held special powers, able to take on whichever form they chose; even a butterfly or a beetle boring into the entrails of a fir tree may well be a spying elf in disguise. Most people who lived near forests dreaded these creatures and were careful not to offend them, lest elfin malevolence afflict them with some mysterious illness.

Storms were a particularly treacherous time for country folk. That was when the *wilden Jäger*, a bespectacled oaf, took his revenge on those who dared laugh at him for once losing his rifle to a clever rabbit. He approached his victims with a piercing cry – *Hu Hu!* – striking terror into their hearts. Also known as the Wandering Jew, it was said he was doomed to roam the earth restlessly until Judgement Day because he had refused to allow Christ to drink from a horse trough, inviting him instead to lick muddy hoofprints on the ground.

Anna's daydreaming was interrupted by a rustling noise in the bushes. Her insides churned. She held her breath, scared of what creature may be lurking, ready to pounce. She could hear the gardener in the distance, whistling as he raked. Should she scream for help? A foot with long claws emerged from the bushes, followed by a scratching sound. To her relief, a shaggy brown hen who had ventured far from the chicken coop poked its head out. Anna climbed down the tree, as silently as she could, trying hard not to frighten the bird away. Once she was on solid ground, she snuck up from behind and reached down to grab it. Expecting a flurry of feathers and clucking protests, she was surprised to find it came willingly. Carrying the rescued fowl, Anna trudged back up the meadow towards where she had last seen the gardener working, past bushes that had been carefully trimmed into the shapes of animals – a bear, a cat, a rooster. She heard him splitting wood and followed a stone path along the side of the house.

'Hello,' she said. 'I found her in the bushes down by the river.' She held the chicken out for him. 'I thought she might be yours.'

The gardener answered with a smile and put down his axe. Taking his time, he bundled the firewood into the wheelbarrow before heading towards a tumbledown woodshed at the edge of the garden. He was old and taciturn, but Anna felt safe in his silence. Still clutching the chicken she followed him, watching as he stacked logs into a neat pile.

'Pop Ella down over there.' He pointed to a chicken coop. 'You're quite good with animals, for a city girl.'

Anna smiled. She had shared her love for all creatures with Mutti, the two of them always stopping to pat a cat or chat to the owner of a dog. On their strolls together around the Englischer Garten, they would watch wild rabbits, foxes and squirrels playing among the trees.

The red door of the shed was wide open, and some hens raced towards them as they approached. Ella started flapping wildly and jumped down to join them. The gardener clucked softly as he reached up to a shelf lined with glass jars and large rusty tins labelled POISON. He took down a bucket of food and handed it to Anna. She tossed scraps to the birds, who eagerly pecked at carrot peels and green potatoes, scratching around in the dirt for loose kernels of corn. Within minutes they had polished off the lot. He came over and waved his arms about like a scarecrow, herding the chickens back into the henhouse, bolting the door behind them with a large rusty nail.

'Some days I like to get the girls in much earlier than usual, especially if naughty ones like Ella have wandered off. The foxes are already likely to have sniffed out their chance for a quick snack.'

Anna followed him barefoot around the old shed. In the far corner, a pile of hay had been stacked against the back wall. The gardener teased out some small clumps, which he placed inside a wicker basket. He handed her a bucket of grain.

'Would you like to help feed the rabbits?'

'Yes, please.'

A large hutch suddenly came to life as rabbits emerged from underground tunnels. As the gardener opened the door they spun around his feet, making eager little grunting noises as they waited for him to toss some hay onto the floor. He called them to him by name, reaching out to pat each one. He let Anna hand them their food while he grabbed a large white male by the scruff of its neck and flipped it upside down. The rabbit lay motionless in his arms, paws frozen in the air, pink nose twitching.

'Meet King Solomon,' he said, 'The father of all rabbits.'

He was a beautiful creature. As Anna stroked his soft belly, the rabbit stared up at her. The gardener lowered him to the ground, and he joined the others who were madly racing around the large hutch, dropping tiny round pellets behind them in their excitement. He picked up a small shovel and started cleaning out a mound of dirt from one corner. In a separate hutch off to the side, Anna noticed a few baby rabbits huddled together. She reached in and lifted one out. It had short ears and silky, white fur. An opaque film covered one of its eyes, the rim red and caked with crusts. She wiped it with her finger.

'Stop!' The gardener had noticed her and came rushing over. He grabbed the tiny rabbit from her, placing it back in the hutch. He led her over to a pump. 'Here, quickly! Wash your hands. There are some nasty chemicals around here.'

'Why are the babies separated from their mothers?' she asked.

'Never you mind,' he snapped. 'Best you run along now. They will be serving lunch up at the house shortly.' He turned briskly, disappearing into the garden.

Anna raced back to the river, where she'd left her belongings in her rush to pick up the hen. She sat down and put on her shoes and socks, and lifted her bag, holding it close to her chest. On her way back to the house, she felt compelled to take one last look at the baby rabbits. She snuck back in and crouched beside the small hutch. The little ones all had bloodshot eyes, watery and opaque, as if they'd been crying. A sign penned in cursive script was pinned to the cage: *Experimental Stock*. There was one thing the young rabbits had in common, beyond their fluffy cuteness. Just like Anna and King Solomon, each one of them had different-coloured eyes.

CHAPTER 10

BIRDUM

MONDAY 26TH SEPTEMBER, 1938

Pat Dougan knocked loudly at the front door. When no-one answered, he made his way around the side of the hotel and tapped insistently on Anna's window. She jumped out of bed and threw on a robe. Pulling the curtains aside, she saw him standing there, dark rings under his red eyes. She opened the window. He leaned in, firing words at her so rapidly she could barely make out what he was saying.

'Gone . . . night . . . disappeared.'

'Slow down, Pat. What are you talking about?'

'It's Max Schmidt.' He took a deep breath. 'Been missing since last night. No-one can find him.'

Anna bit her lip. She spoke slowly, trying to sound calm. 'I'll just get dressed, Pat. Can you meet me out the front in a couple of minutes?'

She threw on some clothes, brushed her hair and rushed outside. Pat was standing beside Fergus, whose face was unshaven and ashen.

'Now, tell me what's happened,' she said.

Fergus lived in the shack next door to Max Schmidt. He took a step closer to Anna and spoke in a soft but steady voice. 'No-one really knows. He was due to leave for Newcastle Waters early today, being a Monday and all, you know, on his usual trip flogging his wares. Well, I saw him getting things ready yesterday early evening, loading up the truck.'

'It was still there in the morning, later than usual,' Pat said. 'Fergus went to check why he hadn't left yet. Couldn't find him anywhere.'

'It was like something gave 'im a huge fright and he just bolted. As if all these clouds approaching scared him off. Left everything where it was, even his dinner. Not that I love the bloke, or anything – don't get me wrong – but that doesn't mean I'd wish the old kraut dead.' Fergus turned to Anna. 'No offence to you.'

'Let's be honest, Fergus – between you and me,' Pat chimed in, 'it wouldn't be such a tragedy to see the bugger go.'

'I know, I know, he carries a lot of spleen, but no-one deserves to die out in the damn bush.'

'How do you know he's dead, Fergus?' Anna asked.

Fergus coughed. 'Well, I s'pose I don't.'

Around noon Officer Strehlow came trudging down the road, the sky behind him a turbid haze. A pistol was strapped to his side.

'Seems his dog's vanished, too.'

The policeman had driven all the way down from Mataranka after receiving a telegram Pat Dougan had sent via Fergus. He waited for someone to say something. Tom O'Hara stood rooted to the spot, wearing tattered overalls and dusty boots. Eyes watery and red, he chewed on tobacco, his arms folded across his chest. Alter swatted mosquitoes from his face. Anna jingled the keys in her apron pocket, her hands trembling. When it was clear no-one was going to speak, the stout officer took the lead, ushering them all inside the hotel to the Lemon and Claret Room. Alter headed straight to the velvet armchair, while Anna sat beside the window, biting her nails. Tom leaned casually against the doorframe, the rest of them lining up along the wall like suspects in some tawdry detective novel.

Strehlow surveyed the room. 'So, who saw him last then?'

Alter fiddled with his bow tie. Fergus didn't open his mouth. Pat stared out the window.

Anna stole a glance at Tom, who was looking down at the rug. She hesitated before she spoke. 'Well, I was planning to go speak to him last night – but I never got there.'

Alter shot a steely look at her that made her recoil.

The officer pounced. 'Do go on, Miss Winter. I'm interested to hear what you have to say. What did you want to chat to him about? At this stage of the investigation, I'd welcome anything that might shed some light on your friend's disappearance.'

'Her friend?' Tom piped up. 'That man was nobody's friend. There isn't a bloke within two hundred miles who doesn't harbour some motive for doing away with Max Schmidt.'

'Hold on,' Pat said. 'Are you insinuating one of us killed the bloke?'

Officer Strehlow glanced at Pat. 'Until I find a lead, you're all suspects.'

'Well then, I might add that I heard Max fighting with these two, not long before he disappeared.' Pat shot a look at Alter.

'That was what I was going to talk to Max about,' Anna blurted out. 'He insulted Mr Mayseh.'

'Is that so?' The policeman turned to Alter. 'And what did you do about that, Mr Mayseh?'

Alter mumbled something.

'Please speak up. None of us can hear you.'

Alter shifted uncomfortably in his chair and looked down at the carpet, quietly repeating what he had said. 'Nothing.'

'Pardon? I still can't hear you.'

'Nothing!' he shouted. 'I did nothing. The *schmock* didn't deserve an answer.'

'What did he say to you?'

'He accused me of being a bloody Jew.'

'And you are sure you didn't respond, get riled up?'

Wasn't that the oldest trick in the world? Frame the Jew as the aggressor to make Jew-hatred seem justified.

'No,' Alter replied.

Officer Strehlow coughed loudly. The Lemon and Claret Room became quiet, and though it was clear no-one was keen to volunteer any more information, he continued his line of questioning.

Strehlow strolled around the room and stopped in front of Anna. 'Where were you at the time of his disappearance, madam? May I ask why you didn't end up visiting your countryman?'

She felt herself blushing, but before she could come up with an answer Alter interjected. 'Because she was with me,' he said with an iron tongue.

All eyes fixed on Alter, who sat there with a smug grin on his face. They shifted their attention to Anna, slowly dissolving her with their stares.

Silence filled the room again. Alter's words seemed to obliterate Officer Strehlow's line of questioning, pushing him onto his next suspect.

'And what about you, Mr O'Hara? I believe the two of you weren't exactly on the best of terms either. In fact, I've heard you were bitter rivals.'

'With all due respect, Officer Strehlow, you don't murder a bloke just because he brews a few lousy hops.'

'Hmm.' The police officer strolled across the room and stood directly in front of Tom. 'You know what? Life has taught me to be cautious.' He turned to face the others, and looked around the room. 'Over the years I've seen people knocked off for lesser things.'

He continued questioning the group until he was satisfied that he had extracted all the information he possibly could. He had spent the late morning prowling about, looking for any signs or clues to Schmidt's disappearance. Some of the Yangman mob had been sent out to search for tracks, but they came back with no leads. There were many ways to go missing from the world, but the Australian outback excelled in mysterious disappearances. Within a mile radius it was possible to succumb to dingoes, wild pigs or marauding green ants. More often it was the very guts of Australia that simply swallowed people up, leaving missing bodies and unsolved mysteries in its wake. The land around Birdum was known by the local Yangman tribe as spirit country, dotted with gaping sinkholes that, according to legend, took revenge on those who would mistreat it. And there were plenty of white men who did that. There were places that warned you away before they claimed you, if you only took the time to listen.

The clouds began to look threatening. In a hurry to get away before any rains bore down, and knowing dinner was waiting for him at home, Officer Strehlow soon left Birdum and its unsolved mystery behind.

As night fell, now feeling agitated, Anna decided to sneak into Max Schmidt's shack to search for some clue, missed by Officer Strehlow, that might explain the man's sudden disappearance. Her silhouette followed her across the road, like the heavy presence of someone relentlessly watching her. What if all these years, Schmidt had been secretly spying on her? She knew it was a ridiculous, paranoid thought, that it overrode all logic – they had never spoken about what had brought each of them from Germany all the way to Birdum. She recalled one of their very rare conversations several months ago, in which he had voiced his support for recent events in Europe.

'It's not so bad they are cracking down on certain people back home. Some have gained way too much wealth and control,' he had said. 'And it's not only the Jews that are a problem. The enormous burden on our Fatherland of the mentally ill, the blind and deaf; all those parasites ordinary Germans have had to support through their taxes. Hitler has a point when he speaks of *Lebensunwertes Leben*. These people's lives are not worth living. They are useless eaters.'

What unseen evil was lurking? If he wasn't a Nazi spy – if in fact, like her, he was in hiding, and they had found him out – then it seemed inevitable she would be next in line. Had they somehow snatched him away in the dead of night? She had thought that in coming to Birdum she would finally be free. But perhaps she was sentenced to a life in which she constantly feared someone lurking in the shadows, ready to pounce when she least expected.

It had taken five years to swallow up the person she had once been. But during the last year headlines screamed from crumpled newspapers abandoned on chairs on the veranda and lying around on the counter inside the pub: Hitler gathering momentum in Europe, all the while promising compromise. Her head sank as she walked, her shadow decapitated. Shivering as darkness crept over the town, she drew in her shoulders, glancing back, unable to shake the constant feeling that she was being watched. Fumbling in semi-darkness, she pushed the front door, which opened onto piles of empty hessian sacks and bottles stacked along the dusty walls.

She wondered where he could be. There was nowhere to hide in this town. She held up her lantern. The curtains were still drawn across his front window, his dinner grown cold on the table, a bottle of beer half empty. The dog's kibble sat uneaten in its bowl. A newspaper lay strewn on the floor, headlines screaming about the Munich Agreement in which the British prime minister, Neville Chamberlain, was rumoured to be ready to agree to Hitler's annexation of the Sudetenland. Tiptoeing down the narrow corridor towards the bedroom, Anna started rummaging through drawers, hunting in vain for some evidence – perhaps a letter in German, or something scribbled on the back of a postcard. A rough blanket was thrown back on the bed, Schmidt's pyjamas tossed aside. She searched through the pockets of a jacket lying on the floor. How could he simply disappear without explanation? Surely he would have left a note somewhere. Her apprehension grew with each passing moment. She felt the urge to move fast, afraid to linger in case someone appeared in the doorway; in this small town, all eyes were watching. The silence was broken only by the staccato ticking of the clock as its hands crept forward. She found nothing.

The rains were rumoured to be particularly violent this year, hurling themselves at the land to announce the start of the wet season. The cruel sun had scorched the land for months on end. A few dry twisted trees seemed to reach out to the heavens, waiting for new life to erupt out of exhaustion. Slender wisps of grey smoke rose from the landscape, the air smouldering with residue.

She imagined Schmidt lost out in the bush, dishevelled, ravenous, his body ravished by mites.

Anna walked back to the hotel, arms crossed, her head bowed. She hadn't noticed Alter standing there on the veranda. He was about to step out of the shadows to greet her, but as she came closer he heard her muffled sobs. Her distress took him by surprise. She stood on the threshold, fiddling with the lock. Alter stayed hidden, breathing quietly, trapped between wanting to hold her and the fear that if he stepped forward he would scare her.

In an instant, all expression drained from her face as she froze like a wild animal sensing danger nearby. Slowly, she turned towards him.

'I know you are there.'

He drew closer, stopping just in front of her. 'Where have you been?' He reached out his hand, but she opened the door and rushed straight towards her room.

CHAPTER 11

LANDSBERG

SATURDAY 24ᵀᴴ MAY, 1924

Professor Jäger was nowhere to be seen. He had called for Anna to come to his study before lunch. While she waited she scanned the shelves of his massive library, towers of books stacked on tables, magazines and newspapers piled up on the windowsill. She plucked out a tome with gold lettering along its spine, and sounded out the letters of the lengthy title: *Auge-närzt-lichen oper-ati-onen*. It was an illustrated book of eye surgery, with a dedication scrawled inside: *To Hans Jäger – my finest student – may you go on to achieve greatness*. It was signed by the author himself, Ernst Fuchs. She turned the pages, stopping at an intricate hand drawing of a woman with short, blonde curls. The model's left eye was blue; a shapely eyebrow arched above it. But where the right eye should have been, a grotesque swelling covered by a web of bulging veins jutted out like a horn. It hung down to reach the corner of the woman's mouth. A pupil floating on the very tip stared outwards as if longing to escape the whole ghastly mess. Anna quickly flipped to the next page, which was filled with an elaborate sketch of a young child with beautiful long braids. The girl's forehead was covered with a knotted, floral scarf under which another bulbous eye bulged out.

'Hello, my dear. I trust you are settling in.'

Anna turned to see the professor standing by the door. Snapping the book shut, she quickly placed it back on the shelf and picked Lalka up from where she had left her lying on the rug. He tossed his hat onto a marble bust and headed across to the desk. Framed diplomas covered the wall behind him. Settling into a chair, he smoothed down strands of greasy hair plastered across his balding head.

'You may continue,' he said. 'That book you were looking at is the bible for us eye surgeons, and the man who wrote it is a genius. He taught me that attention to detail is of the utmost importance in everything you do, especially for my profession. The only organ more complex than the brain is the eye.'

Anna took the book back down from the shelf and continued to look at the drawings, feeling a mixture of revulsion and fascination. She thought about the people who modelled for the artist and wondered what was wrong with them. She squinted as she turned the pages, rubbing her eyes.

'What's wrong, child?' the professor asked, peering over the rim of his spectacles.

'Nothing, sir.'

'Come.' His fingers beckoned, reeling her in like a fish.

She closed the book again and padded across the room.

'Here,' he said, pointing to a chair.

She sat down beside him, hugging Lalka tightly.

'Look at me,' he said, cupping her chin in his hand.

She sat still as he turned off the lamp. He shone a torch in each eye, then pointed in front of her. 'Follow my finger.'

The bright light, coupled with the stench of stale tobacco on his breath, made her eyes water. He showed her a chart filled with black letters and asked her to read the bottom line. She struggled to make out the blurry characters. She closed her eyes, only to see images of the letters still flashing before her.

He grabbed a small brown vial from the desk. 'Lean back, please. I am just going to use some drops so I can see the back of your eye.'

Anna froze. A wave of nausea suddenly engulfed her, and she started dry-retching as she felt a headache brewing. Papa called them her nerve storms, which usually came on when she was upset.

'Here.' He picked up a decanter that rested on the sideboard and poured a glass of water. 'Drink this.'

She took a sip.

Turning his attention away from Anna, the professor hurriedly scribbled some notes into an exercise book. 'I'm only trying to help you, silly child,' he snorted, without looking up. He pulled a hand-kerchief out from the pocket of his jacket and handed it to her. 'Dry your eyes. We will continue the examination some other time. Let me show you something special now.'

He fiddled with the latch of a rectangular box and opened the lid to reveal a collection of glass eyes: twenty orbs of different colours, each staring in a different direction. He lifted one out and placed it in Anna's palm.

'They are far superior to manufactured glass eyes. I have someone who crafts them for me by hand.' He was smiling. He slid a large model of an eyeball towards her from the other side of the desk. 'This one was made especially for me by Fraulein Schilling at the Puppetarium. Such exquisite detail.' He rotated the specimen and poked his finger inside it. 'Only one-sixth of your eye is visible to the outside world. See these muscles here? They work in pairs to pull the eyes in each direction. The ability to rotate your eyeball means you can keep your eyes firmly fixed on the horizon as you tilt your head. Important for focusing on your prey.'

Anna felt submerged underwater, the professor's voice sounding distorted as he droned on, his face blurry.

He picked up a magnifying glass and started to examine a glistening eyeball that lay on a metal tray in front of him that Anna had not noticed until just now. 'My students usually dissect bull's eyes,' he said, 'but I am fortunate myself to have access to human eyes.' He poked at it with the tip of a pair of scissors. 'Fascinating, isn't it?'

Anna looked on, intrigued, although she felt uneasy wondering where the eye had come from.

The professor's concentration was broken by a knock at the door.

'Enter!'

The butler ushered a visitor into the room. The woman had a pasty face and short, oily hair swept into a tight bun. Her pale eyes glinted under thick eyebrows, thin lips drawing a line across a squarish jaw.

'Ah! My dearest Dr Magnussen.' The professor eagerly made his way over to her, holding out his hand. 'So glad you could make it. Good to see you. It's been far too long.'

'It has indeed. What a charming place you have here. And so close to everything.'

He led her over to a pair of leather couches, leaving Anna by the desk. They sat opposite each other, speaking in hushed tones as he filled two glasses with whisky. The visitor was fidgety, her fingers clawing alternatively at the pleat of her grey skirt and the buttoned-up collar of her white blouse. She stole occasional glances at Anna, who was feeling better and had gone back to scanning the rows of musty, leather-bound books lining the shelves, trying to avoid looking at the eye on the desk. The adults' voices droned in the background. She looked at miniature ornaments, bronze statues, muted paintings of sailing ships, a silver candelabra beside a photo of a young girl with a huge bow in her hair. Boredom slowly encroached.

'The rabbits have been breeding very well.'

Anna's ears pricked up.

'That is excellent news, Herr Professor,' the woman lowered her voice to a soft purr. 'I have found a title for my research paper: *The Influence of the Colour Gene on the Development of Pigment in the Eyes of the Rabbit.*'

Anna knocked over the model of the eye she had been looking at. It cracked neatly in two, a rogue shard of clay ricocheting under the desk. The adults were so engrossed in conversation, they didn't seem to notice.

'As I explained in my letter, I already have keen interest in this project from my colleagues at the Kaiser Wilhelm Institute.' The doctor leaned forward in her chair. 'Also, our National Socialist Workers' Party has been very supportive. They understand more than most how crucial this work is, and grasp its potential applications. It is highly relevant to our times, the preservation of the German nation: the very question of which races and peoples should live in future Europe.'

Anna scrambled to fit the pieces of the model back together and return it to the shelf, hoping the professor wouldn't notice the crack.

Dr Magnussen's voice became shrill. 'The Jewish Question is one of our core problems. The Jew, who enjoys hospitality in this wonderful country, is our enemy. None of this can be simply solved by their emigration. We have seen that these types will only create unrest elsewhere and incite other people against each other.'

'I do acknowledge that certain diseases cannot be overcome without surgery,' the professor said.

'You cannot deny this, even though I myself abhor the knife.'

Anna pulled out another book from the shelf and was pretending to read Lalka a story. At that precise moment, Professor Jäger turned his attention to her again. Papa's boss may be a very famous eye surgeon, but the way he seemed to stare right inside her made her wonder if he could also read minds.

'Come over here, my dear.' He patted the cushion beside him. 'And bring that book with you.'

She walked across to him and sat down.

He opened the cover. 'Ah! *Augendienst.* Good choice of reading, my dearest. This is the first textbook of ophthalmology, written back in the 1500s.' He turned to his guest. 'You see, Dr Magnussen, this one already shows an interest in the study of eyes.'

The visitor crossed her legs.

'Let me introduce you to our little Anna. The poor child's mother died not long ago, so I have invited her to join us here on weekends. Her father, Gustav, is my very loyal driver. The man is devastated over his loss.'

The woman leaned across to Anna. 'I can see how much you love playing with your doll.'

'Yes.'

'May I ask what her name is?'

Anna turned Lalka to face away from the woman. 'Lali.'

'She looks very much like you, you know. Would you like to introduce us?'

No, she would not.

The woman held out her hand. 'She's an unusual little thing, isn't she?'

It wasn't clear if she meant Anna or her doll.

'She has such interesting eyes. They are different colours, just like yours. May I?'

The woman reached across and tried to grab Lalka away from her, but Anna held on tightly.

'Wouldn't you like her to have two beautiful blue eyes? We could easily fix the faulty one with some magic drops.' She winked at the professor and whispered, 'Adrenaline works wonders on eye colour.'

He leaned back and stretched his legs.

She looked across at Anna again. 'Lali. What a strange name to choose for a doll. Why don't we change it to a good, solid German name, like Helga – or maybe Gerda?'

At that moment the clock sounded twelve, followed by a knock at the door.

'Yes?' The professor finished what was left in his glass.

A maid came in and stood before them.

'Lunch will be served shortly.' She spoke softly.

Lalka's introduction to the lady doctor was soon forgotten.

'Have you lost your voice, Gisela?' Professor Jäger said dryly.

The young woman's cheeks turned red.

'I seem to spend my life nowadays telling my servants how to do their jobs,' the professor said.

His visitor laughed politely.

'But you are different, Dr Magnussen. A hard-working and

honest woman. What I like most about you is that you don't harbour any fear. Shall we have another?' He poured some more whisky.

It was Dr Magnussen's turn to blush as they clinked glasses.

'*Prost!*'

He waved at Anna. 'Run along now, my dear child. I will be dining with my colleague today. You may go join your Papa. I believe he has some errands to run at the Puppetarium after lunch.'

Anna left the room, hugging Lalka. She stood in the hallway, trying to listen in on what they were saying. Were they talking about her? The woman had been staring at her in such a strange way.

The professor spoke loudly. 'Dr Magnussen, like me, you are a doctor of the highest integrity and I know I can trust you whole-heartedly.'

'Of course. I am at your service, professor. The child will be an invaluable asset to our project.'

'Thank you. I do look very much forward to collaborating with you on this study.'

'What will you tell her father?'

'Don't worry. You can leave all that to me. I will take care of it. As I said, Gustav is devoted to me.'

'Yes. But he sees everything – it's those I trust the least.'

On her way back to the dining room the maid brushed past Anna, who had tucked herself in behind a coat stand. Taking shallow breaths, Anna stayed perfectly still until she heard the woman's footsteps disappear down the hallway. Just as she was about to sneak out of her hiding place and run up to her room, she heard someone open the front door and make their way towards the study. There was a knock, and the professor called from inside: 'Enter!'

Anna peeked out from between the coats. The gardener stood there just long enough for her to catch a glimpse of a familiar jar he held tucked under his arm. It was filled with tiny rabbits' eyeballs.

CHAPTER 12

BIRDUM

TUESDAY 27TH SEPTEMBER, 1938

Hot winds gave way to occasional drops of rain. By Tuesday, lightning flashed over the land. The sun grew weaker as clouds continued to gather, a fresh breeze teasing the shrivelled trees. Inside the pub, Alter's notebook lay open at one end of the counter, with its half-lines, scribbles and words jumbled or crossed out. Even though this was only his fourth day in Birdum, he had already begun to grow languid. The train was due to arrive early Friday evening. He was neglecting his poetry, jotting down ideas for an essay instead. How to distil all he had seen since leaving Europe? And what to make of these fantasies he harboured, of a land open to welcoming refugees? The idea had taken hold of him – a dream insistent on breaking into his daylight musings.

The locals had tried to ply him with beer. 'Drink up! Our shout.'

After a few ales Alter's pale face turned ruddy, blue eyes glinting. Standing on his chair, he burst into song. No-one understood the words but they all clapped along, clinking spoons on their glasses with gusto. For the duration of his performance he became one of them, privy to slaps on the back and hands clamped onto his shoulders. Not long after the final note they all retreated to the bar and Alter went back to being the stranger in the far corner again. Preoccupied with his own visions, he wrote furiously in his notebook – as if he had some urgent, secret message to record.

In the muted light of dusk, the pub seemed populated by propped-up corpses, the fug of cigarette smoke and humidity shrouding everything in a funereal pall. The furniture was arranged to give a sense of permanence – the display cabinet against the wall, the posters and trophies behind the bar. After the last of the patrons had left, Anna sat herself down beside Alter. She picked at a plate of greasy food. A man of words, he was uncomfortable with her silence. Everyone he knew loved to spew forth their stories and opinions. Strange now to try and make sense of someone who was so reticent to reveal her inner workings.

'Tell me.' He placed his hand on hers.

She moved her hand away, reaching for the salt shaker, which went crashing to the floor. Alter bent over and picked it up.

'Tell you what?' She chewed on a gristly piece of bacon.

'What makes you so afraid and sad?' he asked, placing the salt back on the table.

Tears welled in her eyes. Alter prayed for them to rain down from her cloudy past. 'Nothing.'

'Why were you so rattled by Schmidt? You went to his house last night, didn't you? What were you looking for?'

Alter hoped that at least some wordless exchange between them – a pause, a look askance – would reveal this woman to him.

'We're closed now,' she said, wiping a tear away with her napkin.

Pushing her chair back, she stood and started clearing tables, methodically stacking dirty plates and cups onto a tray. He got up to leave. With her back turned towards him she asked if he had an umbrella.

'No. What for?'

'To go for a walk together.' She dived behind the counter and pulled one out. 'The rain could come any moment now. You've heard them talking about the build-up.'

Placing his hat on his head, he slung his bag over his shoulder. He flicked the umbrella open and held it up as they stepped outside. He looked up at the sky. A full moon, pockmarked and imperfect, stared down at them between the encroaching clouds.

'Rain?' He laughed out loud.

'You've never experienced a wet season, have you?'

Smoke rose into the sky from a nearby campfire, voices wafting across the plains carrying ethereal words and sounds. This country, he had been told, held so many languages. As he listened to the distant voices he feared these too, were doomed to disappear. Many beautiful languages around the world were being gradually cannibalised. An ancient tongue spoken for over five thousand years would have died, if it were not for those who clung to what they saw as the word of God. Since then, a pastiche passed through the lips of Jews wherever they roamed, a babel of dialects and utterances tacked together like barnacles. Worldly words, used for laughter, tears, arguments and making love. Ghost words scattered by stray winds, sinking into the quicksand of time. Lullabies sung by generations of mothers to their trembling infants – *Bey meyn kindele's vigele, shteyt a klor veys tsigele* – a child's wagon guarded by a small white goat.

They walked on together in the comfort of their own silence, Anna herself not ready to talk, which left Alter to his own thoughts on the language of his people. While the ancient language of Hebrew never disappeared from Torah, the written law, Yiddish emerged alongside as its companion, a *tsekrokhene* phoenix, hobbling on one leg. It borrowed orange wing feathers from German, red tail feathers from Russian, green chest plumes from Polish, and a white wilted crest from ancient Aramaic. Scholars argued about where this odd language originated – some were convinced it was from the West, an outgrowth of Bavaria, others were determined to prove it had its origins in the medieval Turks who converted to Judaism hundreds of years ago, settling in the East. But it didn't matter to Alter where Yiddish came from – he was more concerned with where it was headed. For him, Yiddish was a language that emerged as a dance between seclusion and contact with the outside world. It was always regarded as inferior to the Holy Tongue of the Bible, but he was determined to help change all that. A culture lived and breathed and survived through its language. There was a Welsh word he had heard of, *hiraeth*, that described the longing for a home to which one cannot return, a home that maybe never was – the nostalgia, the yearning, the grief for the lost places of one's past. Even though there was no specific word for this in Yiddish, the very notion was embodied in its soul.

Languages, Alter had come to understand, differed not in what they *could* say, but what they *must* say. Yiddish had the dead embedded in its very essence: it was impossible to mention a person who had died without saying *zichrono livrocho* – may their memory be a blessing. It was a language of howled vowels – the *oys*, the *veys*, the *ay-ay-ays* – claimed and spoken by Jews scattered across Europe. There is no such thing as a foreign tongue if you have no home. But he was like a turtle: everywhere he went he carried his home on his back.

After a short stroll from one end of Birdum to the other, they returned to the hotel and each went to bed. Sleep evaded Alter, and he lay awake through the night watching silhouettes of thrashing branches outside his window until grey light made its way around the edges of the curtain. Garrulous magpies began to gossip the morning's news, joined soon after by a choir of feathery tumult. The humidity was oppressive. No gentle spring here; no winking violets or crocuses nodding their heads in the breeze. No spongy, manicured lawns or billowy pines. There were only two seasons in this far-off land: the wet and the dry. There had been much talk about the rains coming so early this year. The earth had been hard and dry for months, thirsting for the first proper downpour. Clouds gathered and swelled. The air throbbed with heat, distant thunder promising an approaching storm.

Alter rose, went to the desk and scribbled across a sheet of yellowed paper in his notebook. Ink-splotched words like tortured souls ran away from his pen. Such a strange alphabet – a collection of hieroglyphics, written from right to left across the page. Sometimes he paused, his hands trembling as he closed his eyes. He had told Anna he was drawn to adventure but, seated at the rickety desk now, he seemed more a victim of his own overconfidence. His peregrinations around the globe, in an ever-widening spiral, seemed fuelled by a childish sense of poetic hope. Yet when he shared his ideas, he saw the contagion of his excitement in her eyes. She hadn't even mocked him when he asked for a plate of boiled potatoes, already a laughing-stock among the men since his arrival when he declared himself a proud vegetarian.

Yes, he knew he was a little odd, but he sensed that Anna felt drawn to him. He felt sad to be leaving her. Looking out the window, he recited poems to an empty vista. Out here, you could become someone new – whomever you chose to be. There was no-one to prove you wrong.

CHAPTER 13

LANDSBERG

SUNDAY 25TH MAY, 1924

'Tell me about the rabbits, Papa.'

The car swerved for an instant before Gustav Müller straightened the wheel again.

'What rabbits, sweetheart?' he felt his throat tighten.

'The ones down in the gardener's shed.'

'Oh, those.' He took a deep breath. 'What would you like to know?'

'The gardener let me help feed them. They are so sweet.'

'Oh. Did he?' He cleared his throat. 'That's nice.'

'But the baby bunnies look so sad, as though they've been crying. Why are they kept apart from their mothers?'

'I'm not sure. Perhaps the professor is trying to breed them?' After a pause, he added, 'Sometimes it is easier not to look at things we do not wish to see.'

Anna wasn't sure what Papa meant. All she could think of was the cute tiny rabbits. 'Do you think he might give us one to take home, Papa? I would love to have a bunny of my own to play with.'

'Where would we keep a rabbit in our apartment, Anna? And besides, who would look after it while you are at school?'

Anna sat staring out the window as they passed the town square. Papa drove down a familiar laneway and parked the car in front of Pignataro's Puppetarium.

'Come along,' Papa said, straightening the feather in his hat as he glanced in the mirror. 'I have a little surprise for you.'

It took a while for Anna's eyes to adjust to the dim light inside the cramped shop. In the far corner a woman sat at a wooden desk, her face hidden in shadows, strips of wet newspaper spread out before her. Anna soon recognised her as the same woman who had handed the professor a package the day before.

Papa took off his hat as Anna followed him over to the workbench. He stood waiting for the woman to look up but she continued to ignore them, dabbing a brush into a pot and layering some glue onto a papier-mâché sculpture that she was fashioning into the shape of a cat. The creature was perched on a pair of hen's feet attached to a metal base. The grotesque catbird would likely join other curious figures on display in the shop. Devils sat beside kings, and clowns slumped against princesses. Puppets and dolls lined the walls, wide eyes gazing out into the stillness of the room, waiting for someone to reach up and bring them to life. Shelves were lined with boxes of small body parts, crammed in between mountains of old newspapers. Taking pride of place on the shelf beside the dollmaker stood a miniature toy theatre, with elaborate curtains and a handpainted backdrop. The proscenium was filled with tiny, paper-doll actors dressed in elaborate costumes, all stuck in their perpetual roles. Glass cases were crammed with antique toys, metal clowns, wind-up trains and rusty acrobats standing on their heads, caught mid-cartwheel – souvenirs of a child's abandoned play. They smiled at Anna mutely, each one begging to be rescued and taken home.

On a separate shelf a mini war raged, its ranks of lead soldiers dressed in military garb, fighting rusty battles long forgotten. They were watched over by a saint sporting a cracked smile. Along one wall were rows of smallish costume dolls, each one dressed in the garb of a different country. Holding Lalka, Anna searched the shop for the familiar cherubic cheeks and glassy eyes of the sorts of dolls she loved.

'We don't have many like her.' The woman's voice was raspy. She slowly placed her tools along one side of the desk, staring at Lalka over the top of her grimy spectacles. 'Where is she from?'

Anna felt her cheeks burning. 'Mutti,' she said. It was a precious shell of a word that hid a lost world. 'Just before she died.' She looked down at her feet, her frilly white socks peeking out above scuffed red shoes.

The dollmaker pulled a handkerchief out from the pocket of her paint-spattered apron to stifle a phlegmy cough. 'Ah! Born from the tomb.' She held out her hand. 'May I see her?'

Anna looked over at Papa, silently imploring him to rescue Lalka from being handed over to a stranger. Papa cleared his throat, and the woman glanced up at him quickly before turning her attention back to the papier-mâché catbird.

'We are here to collect a parcel, Fraulein Schilling.' Papa spoke quietly. He looked around as if to make sure no-one else was in the shop. 'And we have one to deliver as well, from Herr Schilling, your father.'

The woman kept working on the sculpture. Silence draped the room. Almost. Anna could hear the toys whispering among themselves as they watched the scene play out centre stage. She cradled Lalka, hoping she would fall asleep and not have to hear the other dolls laughing at them.

'Your doll's eyes might be closed, but she can still see.' The woman muttered, as if talking to herself.

Lalka's eyes opened with a startled stare as Anna held her upright again. A box of tiny legs lay on the floor. The dollmaker pushed her chair back and bent over to pull a small hessian sack out from under the bench. She slipped a parcel inside and tied it firmly with some string.

'Here you go. It's yours,' she said, sliding it across to Papa.

'We both know it's not mine, Fraulein Schilling.' Papa pulled out a small package from the inside pocket of his jacket and placed it in front of her.

She scooped it up quickly and hid it under the desk.

Papa turned to Anna. 'Darling, Fraulein Schilling here has kindly offered to let you stay with her this morning, while I run some other important errands for the professor.'

Anna looked up at him, feeling uneasy. She did not want to be left alone with this stranger, but already guessed from the stiffness in his voice there would be no point arguing.

'I won't be gone long.' He gave her a peck on the cheek, turned briskly and hurried out.

The quavering sound of church bells crept in from the street as the door swung open and closed. Along one side of the shop where the sun streamed in, the dolls looked a little jaundiced.

'Come! Sit here, child.' The dollmaker patted a faded floral cushion that rested on a chair beside her. 'Nothing to be scared of.' She stifled a cough.

Anna inched forward reluctantly and sat down.

'You know, you have a very special doll,' the woman said, her voice gentler now that Papa had left. 'Your Mutti must have loved you very much. Do you miss her?'

What sort of a question was that?

'The dead never truly leave us, you know,' Fraulein Schilling said airily, as if she had crept inside Anna's mind. 'They are like acrobats balancing on a wire, gliding between life and death. We hold them inside, each one of us a walking cemetery.' Reaching up to a shelf, Fraulein Schilling took down a pert-faced doll with a red mohair wig. 'Let me introduce you to Leisl, my own little girl.'

The doll had a double chin and full cheeks, with feathered eyebrows drawn above blue glass eyes. She wore a white lace dress and clasped a bouquet of dried flowers.

'Liesl was my niece. She died when she was about your age, but she's always here, helping me breathe life back into every doll I work on.'

'Why is she dressed as a bride?'

'As a reminder of what might have been.' She wiped away a tear, straightened her apron and looked across at Anna with cat-green eyes.

'Now, young lady, would you like to learn how to repair a doll?' she asked, changing the subject.

Anna nodded.

'All right, then. But first you must learn a little anatomy,' she said. 'A butcher needs to know that filet mignon is actually the iliopsoas muscle of the cow.'

Anna grimaced.

'So, too, a dollmaker, my dear. Sometimes a doll may have had an unfortunate accident; it is very important to understand the body parts and how they all fit together. For example, see this torn cloth leg?' She pointed to a rag doll that lay crumpled up in one corner. 'It only requires a bit of stitching to make it sit straight. But if sewn into the wrong spot, the whole body will twist.'

She grabbed a doll's head from one of the boxes under the bench and picked up a tool that looked like it came from Mutti's old manicure set.

'This is a beveller. We use it to set eyes.'

She stuck a glass eye on the twisted metal hook poking out from the end.

'When you put it in you want it to lie in the midline. Sometimes it can take hours to find the exact setting. I like to work on both eyes at the same time, because that way the doll can show me itself if something isn't quite right.' She held the doll's head up to the light. 'This is how you check if the whites are equal. You can also see if the eyes are slightly different colours. If the eyes don't quite match, that can really throw you off.' She looked across to Anna. 'Although your doll's eyes are very beautiful, just like yours.'

Anna smiled, her wariness fading as she found herself engrossed in the dollmaker's instructions.

'The French have paperweight eyes, and then there's the paperweight wraparounds. Oh, it gets so complicated.' She laughed. 'That's the scary part for a doll specialist – knowing exactly which eyes to order for each doll. Eyes are never created equal.'

She mixed some plaster of Paris with water to form a thick paste. The white spots spattered onto the back of her hand. Adding too much water prolonged the setting time, causing the mixture to ooze through the front of the eyeball. She spread the plaster along the inside of the head and alongside the eyes, which she was careful to hold in place. One dab between the eyes and it was ready to be left to dry. Carefully, she used a toothpick to remove the excess plaster protruding through the front of the eye.

'Once the eyes are set, it's very hard to change the direction in which they are looking. It's very important when you are repairing a doll not to do anything that can't be undone. Would you like to try?'

'Yes, please.'

'Then wash your hands properly. The oil from your skin can attract insects and mildew to the doll.'

Anna walked over to the sink and turned on the tap. Returning to the desk with clean hands, she asked quietly, 'How do you know all this?'

'A very good question.' Fraulein Schilling smiled at Anna. 'The first doll I ever owned was a matryoshka,' she continued. Although she was taciturn with adults, she was very happy to chat to children. 'It was a gift from my father – who is also a dollmaker – when I was a child he often travelled to Russia for work. I was sometimes allowed to help in his workshop, dusting shelves and checking for broken parts. Instead of a salary, he paid me in dolls. When I was older, my father was offered the job as warden at the prison here in Landsberg and, instead of closing his workshop, he asked me to take over the business. He used to repair all sorts of toys, but I began to specialise in antique costume dolls. We soon started to receive interest from overseas, especially the United States; all sorts of collectors writing to us, from the well-to-do to the ordinary.'

'Which of the dolls are your favourites?' Anna asked.

'I don't have any. Each doll is its own person; you just need time to discover the right one. And when you do, it's like finding a best friend. It's my job to breathe a soul into a doll, and what comes out depends on my mood at the time. Sometimes they turn out looking happy, and other times, a little sad. But it's a child's job to bring the doll to life, so it can tell its own story. The eyes are the most important part. Some children are afraid of blue eyes and think the doll is evil. Those with brown or green eyes are always in demand – they are seen as good dolls.' She turned to Anna and cupped her hand around her chin. 'That makes you perfectly balanced.' She smiled.

Time passed quickly and soon the front door swung open again. Papa had returned. He strode over to the workbench. 'I see you have been quite busy in my absence, ladies.'

'You have a beautiful daughter, Herr Müller. I have been teaching her a little about doll repair today. She is very talented.'

Papa pulled another package out from under his coat and handed it to Fraulein Schilling. 'From the princess in the tower.'

She unwrapped it carefully. It was a Spanish costume doll; one of the most beautiful things Anna had ever seen. Fraulein Schilling lay it down on the table and quickly tore off its head. Anna gasped in horror.

'Anna,' Papa said. He nudged her towards the front of the shop, shielding the bench from view. 'Won't you show me the puppets over here?'

Anna heard Fraulein Schilling scraping and banging as she worked. After a short while she called across to Papa. 'It's done.'

He turned and walked back to the workbench, Anna following. The doll's head was neatly sewn back on.

'Would you like to keep her safe?' Fraulein Schilling asked Anna. 'She is very precious.'

'May I?' Anna looked at Papa.

He nodded. 'Well, I suppose there's no harm in that. She is no longer of any use to us, Fraulein Schilling. Correct?'

The dollmaker's face turned to stone. Anna noticed her fold a small scroll of paper and place it in an envelope, which she tucked inside her pocket.

Papa placed his hand on Anna's shoulder. 'Keep her close and take good care of her.'

He turned to Frau Schilling and whispered: 'You'll make sure the note is delivered on time? We don't want to arouse any suspicion.'

Anna pretended not to listen to the adults as she introduced her new doll to Lalka.

'I'm good at my job. You don't need to question me, Herr Müller.'

'My apologies, Fraulein Schilling, but it's hard to know who to trust nowadays.'

'I understand my father's position as prison warden makes it difficult for you, but I have chosen a different path, as you are well aware. Most people would just rather be pulled by strings from above. That way, they are not to blame for any of their actions.'

Papa lifted his hat. 'Thank you for what you do, Fraulein Schilling. *Auf Weidersehen*.' He ushered Anna towards the door as she cradled both the Spanish doll and Lalka in her arms.

She turned to say goodbye, but the dollmaker had already slid the catbird sculpture in front of her again and was busy applying a layer of glue to its mouth.

CHAPTER 14

BIRDUM

WEDNESDAY 28TH SEPTEMBER, 1938

By Wednesday morning more clouds had rolled into Birdum, resting heavily on the earth. Giants with massive torsos, they wore scowls across their grey faces, hiding the sun as they crept closer and closer to the ground before bursting with rain. Kites who had been gliding in luxurious circles tilted their wings, shrieking pitifully as the ferocious winds and downpour buffeted them off course.

Alter had dreamt of hands rising out of the waters, clasping each other, fingers intertwining to form the roots of a twisted tree that grew to reach the heavens. He scrambled up the trunk, taking all day to climb towards his destination. Once he got there he was forced to turn back, God telling him that he was a pathetic Jew.

'Go to Hell!' said God. 'The quota for Jews up here is already filled.'

Beside him on the veranda, two Yangman women sat propping up an elderly man, surrounded by several children with festering sores on their skin. In the murky light they reminded him of families he had seen on his visits to poverty-stricken *shtetls* in

Eastern Europe, huddled in the doorways of huts, surrounded by the small bundles, lamps and bare utensils of their existence. The children stared at him as he walked past.

Alter went inside hoping to bump into Anna, but the pub was deserted. He wandered out back to the kitchen where he thought he might find her preparing lunch, but the pots stood empty on the stove. It seemed odd that she wasn't around attending to her chores at this time of the morning. He opened the back door and was greeted by a huddle of clucking chickens. Anna had looked exhausted yesterday. Perhaps she had slept in? Alter had been awake half the night, worrying about how spooked Anna seemed by Max Schmidt's disappearance. He made his way down the corridor and knocked gently on her door, but there was no answer.

Heading back to his own room, he gathered his notebooks and papers, tucked his typewriter under one arm and wandered down to the Lemon and Claret Room, deciding to spend the morning on a series of poems he had been working on about Spinoza. It was around the time of his bar mitzvah that he had discovered the famous philosopher, who made a living as an optical-lens grinder of microscopes and telescopes. Instead of attending classes with the rabbi to prepare him to become a man, Alter took to secretly visiting Yankl Veltkraft – a school friend who had a large shelf of worldly books in his house. The boy also had a terrific memory. He would ask Alter to open any poetry book and read the first line of a poem out loud, whereupon Yankl could recite the remaining verse off by heart. Yankl told Alter that according to Spinoza, God and the world were one and the same. This made sense to Alter's young brain as he slowly emerged from the silken web of child-hood. He knew it to be true: had always felt the presence of God in a crow, or a blossom, the whispering of the wind, the sweet taste of his mother's compote. Reading Spinoza, he suddenly felt closer to Heaven because it wasn't a place where God hid away from the world; rather, God was in a kitten, a rat, Mottel the beggar and, most exciting of all, inside himself. No-one was less important than the sun or the moon, each person carrying within them some divine attribute.

As a child Alter listened carefully to the rabbi recite the prayers by day, his friends in *cheder*, the local religious primary school, singing along while he himself mouthed the words silently. Somehow he believed that if he didn't say them out loud, God wouldn't notice him and might skip onto the next boy, upon whom He would unleash His fire and brimstone. Every festival, the boys would whip themselves into a frenzy and chant loudly as they banged their fists on wooden desktops: *L'shana haba'ah b'Yerushalayim*. Next year in Jerusalem. Alter didn't understand what all the fuss was about – why not Warsaw, or Quito, or maybe even Buenos Aires? What did it matter where? Anywhere would do to take in a few miserable Jews looking for shelter.

But what a disobedient world this had become, ready to abandon its inhabitants to their fate. Anyone who thought Europe was still a gentle place of streams, mountains and fairy-tale castles was mistaken. He wished now that he could pray, but despite being steeped in Jewish learning as a child, somewhere along the way he had lost God. Dreams replaced deity as he grew stronger in his determination to be a small saviour in the here and now. He refused to wait for some Lord of All Things to play a vast, silent game of power over those in need. He would be the one to act, to find refuge for himself, and maybe some of his family and friends, all of them hated so virulently just because they were Jews.

He was mired in his thoughts when, to his surprise, he looked up to find Anna curled up in an armchair in one corner of the Lemon and Claret Room, reading a book.

'Oh! Here you are.'

She looked up. 'Where should I be?'

'I've been looking for you.' He sat down on a couch beside her. 'I was worried.'

'About what? I'm fine. There was no need for you to trouble yourself.'

'What are you reading?'

She marked her place with a finger and held up the spine. *Capricornia*. 'It's a brand-new novel. Just been published. Tom brought it back with him from Darwin last time he was there.'

'What's it about?'

'From what I've read so far, it's looking at the appalling way in which white people have conquered this land. Not to draw too many parallels, but it reminds me a little of the way your people have been treated back in Germany.'

They sat together, surrounded by shelves filled with the scribblings of a host of English visitors to Australia. Anna had read them all over the five years she had been in Birdum. They were, in the main, books filled with tragic sentimental travelogues, certain that the opening-up of the interior by pioneers would afford the advance of civilisation. Bush ballads and adventure novels written by those with urban imaginations who took voracious bites out of the landscape, regurgitating them as fodder for city dwellers and armchair adventurers. She abhorred the clichés of lost children, marauding blacks and tall handsome horsemen they wrote about in their celebration of the outback. Journeys by horse, camel, bicycle and aeroplane littered the stories that audiences seemed to crave. They celebrated clearing the ground to spread 'progress' to the furthest reaches, using pet names for the unfamiliar land – the Never Never, the Dead Heart, Back O'Beyond – all hallowed by capitalisation. And placenames reflected either a longing for the pastoral landscapes of Europe and Britain – Newcastle Waters, Pine Creek, Victoria River – or else stood like tombstones for tragic heroes who had sought to explore the unknown – Mt Hopeless, Starvation Lake, Mt Desolation – where they perished from exposure, hunger and thirst. In these books she could see some similarity with the stories of her youth, where tragedy and violence were woven intimately into folklore. Anna had grown up reading fairytales that were populated by ogres and witches, hiding in wait for innocent children who wandered haplessly into dense forests.

It occurred to her that each white man in Birdum seemed to think of himself as a brave pioneer, whether prospector, trader or miner. The adversity faced in living in such a remote environment was heavily romanticised. They became larger than life in their missives home where, had they remained there in the first place, they would probably have disappeared into their own dull lives. And the newspapers reported who was hatched, matched and dispatched, often elaborating on every detail of the person's family tree. The gossip column would list anyone by name who so much as entered or left Birdum, by train or truck. Yet if a black man died it was barely afforded a mention. When a Yangman tribal elder man was struck by lightning last year at Mainoru Station, all that was recorded was that he *bled at ears and nose, rendered unconscious, but later recovered.*

Alter interrupted her thoughts: 'We could be the ones to build a utopia here together, you and me.' His voice trembled with excitement. 'Imagine – a Jew and a German breaking all boundaries. We could help the poor native people too.'

'And how do you propose to do that, exactly?'

'We could teach them agriculture.'

'Ah, but there's the problem, Alter. You see them as exotic, yet still think they are primitive. You can't have them as both. They are human beings, just like you and me, who deserve the same amount of respect.'

'But I do worry. Their welfare is a huge problem.'

'You know what the real problem is, Alter?' She slammed the book down on the coffee table. 'The fact that you see them as a problem. How are you any different to the missionaries, the bush gentry or the anthropologists in the way you view them? Can't you see that our dreams are destined to become someone else's night-mares? This place is built on top of their bones.'

'And what would you have me – a wretched Jew – do? Impale myself upon your high moral arguments? My people are also being persecuted, driven from their homes, their livelihoods destroyed – their very existence threatened. And I have a chance to save a handful of them, Anna. Has that not crossed your mind?'

'Of course it has, but we live here without caring about the past.'

'Why should we look back?' Alter leaned forward in his chair. 'Let whatever ghosts were here sleep peacefully.'

'It is an atrocious silence that echoes in the calls of the wild, of birds who hover above, watching us. You and I sit where the ancient owners of this land once lived, the true name of this place vanished, a country destroyed, its soil mixed with their blood. Rivers and stones hold the silent memories, the heart ripped out of the land. Surely a poet can hear the wind that carries the cries of children beyond time?'

'Yes. But do you think the local white men, filled with such hubris, even read poetry?'

'The people of this land were defenceless against the wagon-loads of people with guns and disease, claiming this country as theirs with such certainty.'

'But you too are an invader. If you feel so strongly, why don't you simply pack up your things and go home?'

She looked at him, dumbfounded. 'I have no home, Alter.'

'Well, I guess that makes two of us.'

He changed the topic abruptly, his speech pressured, as if forcefully trying to lighten the mood. 'I love to travel. In Yiddish we say, *Az men zitst in der heym, tserayst men nit keyn shtivl.* If you stay at home, you won't wear out your boots. Since I was a child, I've always wanted to be where I am not. Although, wherever I am, I feel as though I've never quite arrived. And I don't belong, either.' He paused for a moment, thinking, and then went on: 'My father gave me a beating once when I was a little boy that I've never forgotten. Straight after, my bottom red raw from the memory of his leather belt, I climbed up on the kitchen dresser to try to grab the front-door key hidden inside a sugar bowl. I fell to the ground and as I lay there howling, *I want to go! I'm running away!* My father asked me, *Where will you go?* I remember glaring at him through angry tears. *To the world!* I shouted. 'He opened the door for me, and I ran out into the street. My mother screamed after me: *Do you think there's anything more for you out there than you could find here in Radymno? What kind of joy will being a wanderer bring you? You might as well stay home and help me peel potatoes. We all end up in the cemetery anyway.* I was back home by dinnertime.'

He strolled over to the corner and flicked through the records. He chose one and pulled it out of its sleeve, carefully placing it on the gramophone. The crackle of a big-band recording of the new song 'September in the Rain', by Geraldo and His Orchestra filled the room. Anna picked up her book and hid behind it. Alter shimmied across and peeled it away from her, holding out his hand. Hard as she tried, a smile broke through her scowl, and she let him pull her up from the chair.

'I can be your home,' he said.

They held each other and danced around the room as the singer crooned.

She remembered how she had loved Papa lifting her into his arms and waltzing around the salon, her legs swinging in the air one-two-three in time to the sweet serenade of the violin. Alter danced like a lopsided puppet who was missing one of its strings. Sweating in the airless heat, he hooked his finger under the tight collar of his shirt, loosening his bow tie. He stared into her other-worldly eyes, and kissed her gently.

'*Der ershter broygez iz der bester broygez.*'

'Which means?'

'The first quarrel is the best.'

CHAPTER 15

MUNICH

THURSDAY 19TH JUNE, 1924

Papa sat beside her on the sofa, reading *The Adventures of Pinocchio*, her favourite story. Anna imagined the wooden puppet's nose growing longer with each outlandish lie he told. More than his naughty ways of fakery and deception, it was his yearning to become a real child that fascinated her. For this to happen, Papa explained, he would have to prove himself unselfish, brave and, above all, truthful. But Anna knew real children were nothing like that at all. Anyway, who would want to be a human child? Surely Pinocchio's mechanical reactions were far better than having to feel real heartache? The puppet had to spend hours practising crying, whereas a sea of tears could spring from Anna's eyes in an instant.

The book lay open on Papa's lap. He had fallen asleep mid-sentence, but it didn't matter – they had read it so many times, Anna could recite the story off by heart. She sat still so as not to disturb him; he had been very tired lately. He woke with a start at a sudden knock on the door and threw the book onto the sofa. The pages fell open at a picture of Pinocchio hanging from a scaffold.

Anna thought it was just deserts for the puppet after he behaved so appallingly to his father, Geppetto, who had lovingly carved him out of a piece of enchanted wood. Pinocchio's name meant 'eyes of pine', which made him blind to knowing right from wrong. Anna would never lie to her father.

A woman stood at the entrance of their apartment. She had long eyelashes and red lips, her hair perfectly coiffed. Papa was a good man, gentle and calm, aside from the night following the funeral when he had smashed a mirror, distraught after the loss of his beloved wife. Anna felt safe under the canopy of his love. They didn't need anyone else. But the Lady of the Flowery Dress – carnations, tulips and roses – whom Papa had tipped his hat to in the park during their Sunday stroll last week had brought over a plate of Linzer torte.

Papa bowed awkwardly and invited her in. 'Anna, of course you remember Fraulein Nachtnebel, our neighbour?' He took the woman's fur coat and hung it in the hallway.

She headed straight across the room and draped herself on the sofa. 'You may call me Tantine, my dear.' She smelled of stale cigarettes and wet vegetables, with a hint of lilac perfume sprayed over the top. 'What a pretty dolly you have.'

She reached out to touch Lalka's hair, but Anna refused to give her up. Lalka might be brilliant and strong, but she was anything but *pretty*. Anna was sure, in fact, her doll would consider that description insulting. It made Anna feel doubtful Papa would ever become friends with Tantine. He deplored liars.

It was through Lalka that Anna was learning the rules of the world. She provided answers that none of the adults could. Or would. Lalka was tender and inviting and allowed Anna to fill her with confidences, holding a tiny portion of Anna's soul, protecting and keeping it safe. No. Being pretty was not important.

'Go play in your room, darling. Tantine and I would like to talk privately for a while. I'll be there shortly to say goodnight.'

Anna stared at the plate of cakes on the table, but soon understood she would not be offered any. She cuddled Lalka as she left and went to her room. Busying herself playing with the doll's house Papa had built for her, she filled it with miniature teapots the size of her fingernail and lavish meals fashioned from clay. Tiny things intrigued her, minuscule objects she could fit in the palm of her hand, paintings made from pictures she cut out of old newspapers, gluing matchsticks together to fashion frames. This diminutive home was decorated with hand-knitted rugs for the floors and wallpaper she had painted for each room. Voices and personalities were attributed to dainty stick figures who roamed from the bedroom to the parlour.

Anna was building her dreamland; the life she knew she could never have in full-size. In the world of the doll's house she could imagine the unimaginable, albeit on a small scale, where you could leap about in time and space, visiting a past where the mother of the house was busy in the kitchen frying pancakes that fit on a pinhead. When she placed the small parents on the sofa in front of the fireplace, they stayed there watching the child play with her dolls on the rug. She created a perfect family, in a perfect world of tiny things she dreamt about. Here, the universe obeyed her, and things happened entirely upon her command.

Nothing ever got dirty. Everything was arranged perfectly, with the maid stationed permanently at the entrance, holding a tray of lavishly decorated pink cakes. Life was simpler if it could be contained inside a doll's house. Shrinking her family to the size of ants gave Anna a sense of order. She could keep an eye on everyone's movements and, being able to manipulate this reduced world by imagining grander schemes, she felt there was a clear future for everything.

In the privacy of her bedroom Anna noticed that Lalka seemed quite sulky. She wanted Anna to take the newest toy back to the Puppetarium, because he was mean. But returning Puppet was out of the question. He was a gift from Fraulein Schilling. Besides, Anna hadn't been home when it all happened. The dolls invariably became bored when she was away at school and got into fights that she wasn't there to referee. And Puppet held a frightening sadness; the thought of letting him go made Anna feel like weeping. He would sit slumped over, his head bent forward, deflated after trying so hard to make Papa laugh. And although she loved Lalka with all her heart, it would be a terrible wrong to betray him.

Lalka sat stiffly, her eyes flaming. The bedside lamp hissed.

'What did he say to you?' Anna whispered.

The doll leaned forward, placing her hands on her hips. 'He told me that I'm not real.'

Just then Papa opened the bedroom door. He smiled at Anna and her now lifeless friends, who had instantly swallowed all their words at the sight of an adult. The monkey drummer froze, his mottled fur exposing the tin skull above his right eye. The three-legged donkey cast a giant breathless shadow on the wall.

'It's late, my darling. Time for bed.' He stood at the door, as he did each evening, whispering: 'Goodnight, sweet dreams, see you in the morning'.

Always the same chant, his hand gripping the doorknob as if he were scared to enter or in a hurry to get back to whatever he had been doing.

'Have you chosen which doll to take with you to Landsberg tomorrow?' He stood motionless, his face unshaven.

'Yes, Papa.' She stretched her arms out and yawned. 'Lalka.'

'Of course, my sweetheart.' He turned off the light and closed the door quietly as he left.

Anna never left Lalka behind. Reaching for her in the dark, she dragged her into bed. She threw her arms around the doll, the trembling air of nightfall filling the room as she slowly drifted off to sleep. Anna tossed and turned, falling in and out of dreams. Who to leave behind when they went to Landsberg for the weekend? She faced the same dilemma at the end of each week. How to choose between her trusted companions of the heart? They knew her so well, each one an avid listener to different parts of her life. She read books to her toy Siamese cat, Lungri, his fur thinning where she rubbed him under the red kerchief tied around his neck. His tail was permanently bent into the shape of a question mark. He loved listening to stories from the wild, especially of the great Shere Khan, the rightful chief of the jungle, with whom he shared a nickname because of his shrivelled leg.

When Anna played with each of her dolls, they opened up to reveal a secret life. All except beautiful Luba, who sat silently on her side of the shelf, blonde plaits peering out from under a velvet hat threaded with shiny beading, her white crinoline frock perfectly pressed. Unlike Lalka, who wore a simple straw hat, she was not made to be played with. Although Anna admired Luba, every time she looked at her cold stare she knew that it was Lalka she loved with all her heart.

Each morning when Anna woke, she was amazed to find the toys in the exact same places she had left them the night before. They had moved around so much in her dreams. Dolls were her circle of true friends, each one with a full storied and colour-ful life. They held her world in their petite bodies, whispering and singing as they stomped, danced and paraded around her room. She would never agree to take just one of them, would hide them in her bag, under her hat, in the pocket of her clothes. But who to choose? And how to leave behind the friends she had spoken to every single day of her life, cut them off like dead wood and abandon them like tombstones in what would soon become the cemetery of her room for the entire weekend? They had built a world together; they knew her more perfectly than anyone else. She wanted to speak to each one, tell them she would soon return. Pengi, with his half-open beak, couldn't seem to find the word for goodbye. She lowered her eyes, felt her lips turning numb.

Despite her love for Lalka – her most secret desires and imaginings poured into the hollow vessel of the doll's tiny body – Anna always felt a quiet superiority that lay somewhere between parent and prison officer. They had faced each other across the same bedroom for a year now, but despite the veneer of Lalka's docile smile Anna sometimes thought she saw a slumbrous menace tucked away behind those glass eyes. She was a blank slate onto which Anna could reveal her innermost thoughts and yearnings. Sometimes she spoke to her as if talking to a friend who knew her better than she knew herself. And yet, for all this, there were times she felt as though an empty shell stared back at her. It was on those days the loneliness crept in, bringing on one of Anna's nerve storms. The nausea turned her stomach, jagged pain dug through her skull, and every sound bored straight into her brain. Colours bled into black. After the agony had leeched away her lifeblood for several hours, the distant world would slowly begin creeping back in, spilling around the edge of the floral curtains, the light seeping into Anna's eyes again.

That night, Anna woke to hear the clock in the hallway chiming eleven. She reached out to cuddle Lalka under the covers, but her doll wasn't there. Groping at folds of bedding, feeling around for the familiar coarse curls, the dimple on her tiny chin, Anna's heart started pounding. She grabbed a pillow and threw it aside. Still no Lalka. The light from the landing crept into her room. Kneeling on the floor, she reached under the wooden frame of her bed, searching for the familiar little body. Her panic began to rise when Lalka didn't appear. It felt strangely like she was losing her mother all over again.

She opened her door and crept down the hallway, barefoot. Papa was in the kitchen, standing by the sink, washing dishes. Smoke hung heavy in the air but there was no sign of Tantine, except for a pile of lipstick-stained cigarette butts resting in an ashtray on the table. At the other end, Lalka lay on her back, naked. Her dress, dripping wet, hung over the back of a chair. Anna let out a scream, unsure if she was still inside one of her nightmares.

Papa turned instantly, holding a soapy plate. It slipped from his hand and shattered on the floor, tiny pieces flying off in all directions.

'Careful, Anna. Don't step over here. You'll cut your feet.'

'What have you done to Lalka?' Her words squeezed out between sobs.

'It's all right, darling.' His voice sounded small. 'She's fine. I was just giving her a little wash.'

She wanted to grab Lalka and run to her room, but she froze, watching Papa as he dried his hands and calmly swept up the mess. When he finished, he walked her back to bed, his hand resting on the back of her neck. This time he didn't stay at the door; he followed her and watched as she climbed under the covers, tucking her in tightly as if signalling she was not to escape.

'Why did you take her without asking me?' She could barely contain her anger.

'I'm so sorry. I wanted to surprise you by having her clean and looking her best.'

'Promise you'll bring her back to me soon?'

'Of course I will. But first I need to see that your eyes are tightly closed, young lady.'

She curled up in a ball and made fists, trying to stop herself from trembling.

'Goodnight. Sweet dreams. See you in the morning.' To her surprise, Papa bent down to kiss her, then quickly left the room.

She tried to fall asleep as fast as she could, hoping that when she woke in the morning Lalka would be by her side again.

CHAPTER 16

BIRDUM

THURSDAY 29TH SEPTEMBER, 1938

Wet dawn. The wind moaned. White lightning hooked itself violently into the land. Overnight, the sky had cracked open entirely, rain spilling like grey ink onto parched earth, filling holes that gaped with thirst. Balding, shabby eucalypts swayed their arms violently in both greeting and fear. Lizards hid in the crevices of floorboards on the hotel veranda.

His eyelids heavy, Alter felt fearful of what daylight might bring. What had started as a dance led to a kiss, and this morning he found himself sitting on the edge of the bed in the aftermath of making love to Anna. Would it be delight or shame that hung over them both? He heard her softly calling his name and, turning to face her, found himself once more in her arms. He had known her less than a week but in that time felt a longing for her he never thought possible. He cursed himself, wishing he believed in a God who might hear his anguish too. A German woman with no history. For all he knew she could be a Nazi spy. He prayed to himself, to the long-dead, to anything or anyone who might assuage his fears, to soothe this ridiculous angst. He wept to think the only true peace he would ever know would be when he was a mere handful of dust inside the grave. He was overreacting. She could never wish him any harm; Anna was the embodiment of compassion.

A blowfly circled the ceiling in its noisy attempt at escape. They lay together in Anna's narrow bed as dawn light melted through the curtains. Her girlish shyness crept back after a night in which their craving for each other's bodies had hardly let them sleep. He kissed her again, the stubble on his chin scraping against her cheek.

'Tell me about before.'

Such an awkward question to throw into the stillness after such a storm. He was tugging at shadows, trying to fill in the vague outline she had given him. A bird called urgently outside, raising an alarm.

'Why conjure up the past? I'm happy here.' She listened to the words sneak out from her.

He tickled her belly. 'You're a bad liar, you know.' He was prising open a door she was determined to keep shut.

She slapped him playfully. 'And you are a thief who would mine a person's life just to craft a poem.'

Leaning across, Anna stroked Alter's cheek. They kissed. His mouth, which a moment ago had looked small and vulnerable, turned into the jaws of a hungry animal, demanding and devouring. It was a welcome distraction. Anna was not one for intimate revelations; she excelled in evasion. Instead, she spoke to him with the language of her body.

It was almost 7 a.m. when they woke again. She got up to dress, leaving him sprawled out under the covers, the heat of his body still imprinted on her skin. Anna was a mystery to Alter – he sensed some abysmal loss at her very core. She had given him a thumbnail sketch – her mother had died when she was seven, leaving her alone with her father. And then there was the boat trip to Australia. He caught her reflection in the mirror. He suspected that all she had known back in Europe was lost forever. How could he possibly see what she carried in her depths? Working behind the counter in the hotel she showed a lacquered friendliness to everyone, struggling hard to conceal the sadness he knew was there.

He stared out at the surrounding scrub that was starting to disappear under a watery landscape stretching as far as the eye could see. Humidity rose from the ground, enfolding everything in its oppressive damp arms. Insects thrummed as flashes of lightning announced deafening rolls of thunder. Dark-grey clouds reflected in Alter's eyes, consuming the blue.

Leaping Lena was due to lurch into the station the following evening. Early Saturday morning he would have been on his way to Darwin, where he planned to stay for a couple of days before heading back to Melbourne. But word came via telegraph the night before that the early start to the wet season, heralded by a sudden heavy downpour, had flooded the town of Mataranka, 100 miles to the north. The train was stuck there after being derailed, and no-one knew how long it would take to get it up and running again. For now, there would be no train until the floods receded.

The rains forced him to change his plans again, or at least that's what he told himself. He was secretly relieved to have the chance to spend more time with Anna. She was a mystery he needed to solve. He was determined to figure out the enigmatic laws that governed this woman he had seemed destined to stumble upon in the middle of the outback. It was a biblical story, this wandering through the desert, the sudden downpour and flooding, swarms of locusts. It seemed possible, in that purgatory of time and space imposed upon them, that he may be able to reach closer to her centre. Another week's delay wouldn't make much difference to his travels.

For the white folk, Birdum was the conquest of a hostile landscape. Built on the banks of a shrunken riverbed, it was born from the dream of a train that would bisect the heart of the country from top to bottom. Alter saw it as a possible safe haven, but Anna thought of Birdum more as a dull mote on an intricate carpet. She had woken in the depths of the shuddering night, long after the lamp had stopped hissing. Restless in her half-dreams, she left Alter lying there fast asleep and padded outside to the veranda. In the storm, she sat shivering as she listened to distant moaning echoing across the bush. She remembered the howling of wolves from the depths of the forest back home. She had thought she could hide away inside this scuffed, silent country and slowly creak back to life. Out here, though, despite the vastness that surrounded her – with its yelps, yawps and muffled whispers – she still felt as though Professor Jäger and his cronies were watching her. She lit the lamp and set it down beside her. A mouse who had been scuttling along the wooden boards suddenly froze, looking straight at her, its eyes strangely opaque, the wide round pupil and muddy iris marooned on an island of white. It glared mockingly, as if to say: *Anna, you are a mouse, not a phoenix.* Alter was chiselling away at her heart, even though she thought it had turned to stone long ago. She had been determined to stand on her own two feet, promising herself she would never take up with a man. Flesh had betrayed her.

CHAPTER 17

BIRDUM

OCTOBER, 1938

Ochre mud covered the floor, stagnant and slippery, thick as paint. Gubbins was howling, pulling at a rope that tied him to a pole. Anna tossed the scrawny dog a chicken wing that he fell upon voraciously. When he was done, he licked her hand and soon curled up and fell asleep, caked in mud.

Anna went out front to the veranda and stood staring at the rising waters that had been urged on overnight by more torrential rain. Almost a month of incessant storms had forced rivulets to surge, forming a lake that almost reached the top of the stairs, lapping at the entrance to the hotel. Heavy mist swallowed the tops of trees. During a short let-up in the downpour Tom O'Hara had waded across to the shed and pulled out a rusty dinghy. He fastened it to the edge of the hotel veranda, where it rocked on its mooring. Leeches swollen to the size of grapes clasped onto his ankles, gorging voraciously on his blood. Anna watched water pour over the eaves like shiny ribbons. She had placed buckets under the roof, the drops tapping out soggy tunes. The land had become an ocean, as if the sea wanted to reclaim what it had once conquered millions of years ago.

Even though there were only a few people left in town, most of Anna's day was taken up by the drudgery of chores – preparing meals, washing dishes, mopping muddy floors. At dusk, swallows darted across the surface of the water, flying low out of the damp mist in a glittering spray of colour. Crows wailed, cockatoos scolded and shrieked, and a hawk circled above, swooping and diving before it vanished back into the darkening sky. Despite the rains, the fierce heat brought with it a turbid anguish. Languid, wrapped in a cocoon of mist, the townsfolk and stragglers lined up along the bar, drinking themselves into a stupor, the pub oozing the pungent smell of beer and sweat. When evening came and Anna had finally finished her work, the last of the patrons stumbling back to their rooms, she stepped out onto the veranda to say goodnight to Alter. She had allowed him to charm her completely. Sitting there holding his evening pipe between his lips, he stared straight ahead.

He looked shaggy, his sleeves rolled up to reveal his forearms scabbed with insect bites. His face was pale, his skin wrong for this climate. The back of his shirt looked like flypaper, covered in huge blowflies. Clouds of mosquitoes cleaved the air.

'One more week of this and we'll all find ourselves drowning in a desert,' he said, smiling. He puffed out a smoke cloud. 'Although if I have to be stuck in this purgatorial pub in a purgatorial town, I'm glad that at least it's with you.'

What he didn't tell her was that he felt somewhat relieved – the rains an excuse for him to stay with Anna.

But Alter couldn't know what fragile goods he was handling. For Anna, a true collector would fall in love with a doll at first sight, despite its missing fingers and damaged head. Rummaging through piles of toys at flea markets or unearthing something buried at the bottom of a box out the back of a junk shop, that crazy moment of exhilaration, when treasure surfaces, was impossible to silence. Her love affair with Alter had begun like that too, emerging in such an unexpected place.

They went inside and he followed her down the corridor. She hung the bunch of keys on a hook behind her door, lit the lamp and climbed into bed fully clothed, too tired to undress. The mattress was hard and thin. Rain lashed against the window, the wind howling through the cracks. Alter sat on a chair scribbling in his notebook. She picked up a book, but soon the words turned blurry. The flame faded in the lamp, crackled, and died out. She lay in the dark, eyes wide open. He climbed in beside her. Soon her wakefulness turned to dreams in which the water rose and flooded the hotel, trapping her inside.

The dog howled. Thunder rumbled overhead, clouds unthreading into a fierce storm. Another night of feverish lovemaking. They hid under the covers to avoid the insistent mosquitoes divebombing their sweaty skin. Two strangers clawing at each other's past, they were intoxicated by their shadows climbing into each other, their sighs an echo of distant shores.

'Does your memoir begin here?' she whispered, 'With us?'

'I guess all voyages have to start somewhere.' He scratched at a bite on his forehead.

'So, do you always make a habit of dipping your pen in the ink of someone else's story before drifting on to the next?' Their histories had collided and the mere thought of this being a fleeting encounter made her feel a little ill.

Alter didn't answer. He wished he could eavesdrop on her thoughts, tiptoe around her brain at night, spying on nightmares that choked her breathing. But the past was obscured by lurid smoke, distorting vision behind the heavy eyelids of sleep. Her kisses were sweet, but she kept her feelings to herself. As she slept, the night was peppered with her quiet sighs. What was it that she did not want anyone to see? And what had cleaved her from Europe?

The morning was still, both rain and wind easing a little overnight. The whirring sound of insects harmonised with the soft drizzle on the foggy window. A quiet sky, dense with cloud, hung over the town in a veil of oppression. Rising at dawn, she found twisted sheets and blankets slumped on the floor. She saw her face in the cracked mirror that was mounted on the back of the door. She had huge black rings under her eyes.

Alter was woken abruptly by a blowfly, although he couldn't be sure the buzzing wasn't coming from inside his head. A blackbird trilling outside the window called to him in a familiar voice: *Come home! Come home!* The wet season exhaled the sour-sweet smell of longing. It would soon be time to leave. Drenched and exhausted, he felt himself gasping like a perch dragged up onto the banks of a river. Even the frogs seemed to be croaking a farewell song. Although he was tempted to stay here with Anna, Birdum had grown too small to hold him. He laughed at the thought, as if it were ever big enough to contain more than a few ramshackle buildings and its transient inhabitants. Once again he was drawn towards the unknown. He shivered with a familiar longing, the wind whistling its lonely song as it rattled at the doors and windows again, clawing to come inside. He was a true vagabond.

Back home, Alter had always thought if there was no other way to earn a living he could become a book peddler. After all, how much does a Yiddish writer earn from his scribblings? He would build a small cart and find an old nag that had been put out to pasture. Even if it limped along slowly it wouldn't matter – there was no rush. Piling up the books, he would cover them with a blanket if it rained. He might also need to sell prayer books and trinkets to keep his horse fed. But what better life for a writer – wandering the countryside and collecting stories for free?

He had once visited an institute in the town of Vilna that housed an archive of Jewish items put together by *zamlers*, hundreds of people from across Eastern Europe who went about collecting objects and documents on all aspects of Jewish life. There, you could find anything, from incunabula, eyewitness accounts of pogroms, to the journals of notable Jewish writers like I. L. Peretz and Sholem Aleichem.

'We are both *zamlers* – collectors – you collect dolls, and I collect stories,' he told Anna, leaning back on the couch in the Lemon and Claret Room later that afternoon. 'A writer I once knew, who called himself Ansky, travelled around the Ukraine for two years before the Great War broke out, visiting old people hidden away in their tiny *shtetls*. Like a true *zamler*, he filled his notebooks with their stories. *Amol is gevezen*, once upon a time, rested upon the lips of all those he spoke to – shopkeepers, tailors, rabbis and streetwalkers alike. A hurricane of Yiddish stories piled up in his notebooks.' He thought for a few moments before he spoke again. 'You and I could do that.'

'Do what?'

'Collect stories. It's not a bad idea, you know.'

'I'm not so sure.'

'Oh, come on, Anna. There are so many odd characters around these parts. But that's not who I'm talking about, anyway. There are others here whose stories must be told.'

'It isn't for us to collect their stories. We know nothing of their culture, their traditions, their rules. It would be intruding.'

'Or trying to preserve what is being lost. Like what I do with my own language. Only Yiddish has no land, no borders. Its only soldiers are its writers, and their only weapons are fountain pens.'

'You should visit Katherine if it's unusual stories you're looking for.' She threw him a line, knowing he couldn't resist being lured into another adventure.

'What's so special about it?'

'Russian peanut farmers.'

'What?' He slapped his thigh. 'Perfect! I must stop there along the way.'

'Why do you love travelling so much?' she asked.

'Why wouldn't I?'

'Why do you always have to answer a question with another question?'

'Isn't that exactly what you just did?'

Exasperating. Endearing. Annoying. Charming. He was all those, and more. Alter was a man who never really spoke – rather, he sang. The cadence of his words followed a melody that rose in a crescendo, then suddenly fell away to a mere whisper. It came from his love of Yiddish.

'When you learn Talmud, the interpretation of the written rules of the Torah, you must read with a melody and study with a tune. The singsong of my beloved Yiddish and its penchant for questioning the questioner are derived directly from this.'

Anna watched Alter's eyes glaze over. He seemed transported to another place, another time.

'You know, being a wayfarer is rather a new enterprise for a Jew.' He wiped his forehead with the back of his sleeve. 'In the olden days, not only was it forbidden to leave home, but going on any kind of journey would entail risking your own life. Yet every generation has its courageous souls, who rise from among the fearful masses and take a gamble when opportunity presents itself. That is the history of my people, from our earliest times. Yes, they were shoemakers, blacksmiths, bakers, butchers, tailors, but there were also those who, by the very nature of their trade, were forced to become wanderers.'

An insect buzzed around his head and he swatted it.

'I'm a poet. For me, nothing is ordinary. Wonder lies hidden in everything; even a stone holds a story. When I travel, I am cut loose from banality and become a voyeur, unable to resist the lure of new vistas that may lie ahead. I feel my vision become sharper; I notice the strangeness of the familiar and the plenitude of the unexpected. I am a child again, bathed in the realm of wonder. I can see the surprising beauty in things; this juxtaposition is living poetry.'

Alter was a city type, a man who had been desperate to try and secure his name among elite literary circles back home. But his eyes betrayed a muted sadness – perhaps from witnessing what was happening across Europe, and seeing too far into the future.

His face turned blank, as if he had dropped a precious vial that contained his excitement. 'I'm afraid it will not bode well for us,' he told Anna.

She looked away, her heart skipping a beat.

'No, no! I'm not talking about you and me.' He placed his hand on hers. 'I meant my fellow Jews back home.'

She felt embarrassed, her concerns over matters of the heart overshadowing his fears for his people. She looked down at their intertwined fingers. It would be fine.

'I feel so safe here with you', he said.

She understood what he meant, the distance from Europe, the seemingly endless space. A landscape so vast, too large for the eye to take in all at once. The allure of this vista – a sky that caressed the earth. But the less you see, the more confident you are in what you have. This place was not untouched, nor was it an empty noth-ingness to fill: the land held deep secrets. Alter felt the siren call of potential, whereas for Anna the land held magic that needed to be protected.

'*Augenblick*', her father would say. It was a game they used to play. She would close her eyes as he spun her around. She felt the world turning. Just as she was about to topple over, he placed his hands on her head to steady her, shouting, '*Augenblick!*' Like a doll, her eyes became the only movable part of her face. She opened them and blinked slowly, photographing in her mind what she saw: a mallard preening its wing, the gardener chopping wood. These moments burned into her memory like a photograph. Years later, stamped into the echoes of time, she could still recall the joy she had felt playing with her father, shrieking with delight as he whizzed her around and around.

The memories folded into each other like a matryoshka, a doll-within-a-doll, the innermost hidden tiny homunculus still recognisable as the exemplar of its kind. Suddenly, it gained a painted-on flourish of a moustache, a pair of thick bushy eyebrows and a familiar, steely gaze – a miniature Professor Jäger. That split second is all Anna ever remembered, and even for that she had to search through a haze of images, looking for what she feared to find. She tried to focus on what he held in his hand.

Her breath slowed as she sat there, her father now a blur at the edge of the frame. The tail of his coat partially obstructed the view – a tiny fleck of the all-too-familiar gingham pinafore, one white ankle sock tucked inside a black shoe. An upside-down blue eye stared back at her, lids wide open, as if begging for help. *Augenblick*. A flash suspended in time, suddenly vanished. Simmering for years, the reluctant memory of Professor Jäger holding Lalka and taking her away slowly started to surface.

'Papa?' she had called. 'Papa!'

Soon she was being carried back to the car, reaching out for her beloved doll. There must have been screams, a hand gagging her mouth as she swallowed her own tears.

'Shh! Shh!' Papa's voice, washing like waves over her terror. 'It will be all right. Lalka will come back to you soon. I promise.'

A little holiday. A trip to see her friends. A visit to the doll doctor for a check-up. He might have said any one of those things. His words had sunk too deep into the bedrock of childhood to uproot. She tried to goad her mind into remembering, but snares trapped the emptiness of forgetting. The pastel-green wall behind Professor Jäger seeped back across the years, his sudden turning-away to hide Lalka inside his coat. It had felt like a little death.

She sat beside Alter on the veranda that evening. The lantern threw long shadows over their faces, surrounding them with an aureole of muted light. They heard something move nearby and sat still, but whatever it was had stopped, or slithered away. Torn corrugated iron clattered against the side of the building. The next morning, she found Gubbins in the corner of the kitchen, lying motionless on his side.

CHAPTER 18

BIRDUM

TUESDAY 18TH – FRIDAY 21ST OCTOBER, 1938

He had hardly slept. A ruined village had appeared in Alter's dreams in a riot of horror and devastation, with blackened timbers and the carcasses of charred animals littering the ground. Lying awake through the night, he had heard Anna calling a name over and over in her sleep. *Lalka*. He watched Anna's silhouette until grey light seeped into the room. Peeling off the covers, he got out of bed quietly. Perched on a rickety chair he picked up his pen, rolling it between his fingers. He watched it move along the page, from right to left, like a soldier grown accustomed to the morning drill. Sitting there, hunched over, his eyes still half asleep, the lines of letters ground to a halt. What was there to say? He slowly wrote a single word, the ink bleeding out like sap from a gnarled tree trunk. He sat still, tracing and retracing the letters.

Anna woke and tiptoed out of bed. Standing behind him, she watched as he carved his pen into the paper, his hand trembling. She reached over to touch his shoulder.

'What are you writing?'

Startled, he dropped the pen.

'I am a poet. I do not write. I search for what is hidden.'

'And what have you found?' She traced the letters with her finger, leaving a smudge of black ink on the page.

A bleak silence hung between them. What more was there to say? She was driving a slow arrow through his heart with her patchy backstory.

'What do the letters spell?' she asked, teasing him.

'A word without a past has no meaning.'

'Tell me what the word is.'

He pointed to each letter as he read out loud: '*Lamed, aleph, lamed, koof, ayin.* It's a name.'

'Is it my name?'

'No. It spells L-A-L-K-A.'

Here they were, on the other side of the world, and it occurred to him that this woman, whose heart he had embraced, leaping across the chasm of difference between them to fall in love, may not be who she said she was.

'You told me your doll's name was Lali. That wouldn't happen to be short for Lalka would it? Your mother gave you this doll just before she died?'

Her smile disappeared. The silence filled Alter with a rotting sense of dread. The rain battered the outside walls and he felt like he was drowning in confusion.

'*Lalka* is the Polish word for doll. You were mumbling it in your sleep, Anna.'

He would give her the benefit of the doubt. Perhaps there was some Eastern European bloodline on her mother's side she had forgotten to mention. Or could it be possible that her mother had been Jewish, an onerous secret she had taken to the grave?

Maybe there was a simple explanation and Anna just wasn't aware of the origins of her treasured doll's name?

'You must have misheard me.'

Despite her surprise at learning the meaning of Lalka's name, she wasn't going to betray the promise she had made to Mutti before she died, to keep the real name secret.

'Lalka means "doll" in Yiddish too.' He paused for a moment to make sure his revelation had sunk in. 'I wonder why a German woman would utter a Yiddish name in her sleep.'

It had never crossed Anna's mind to question the origins of her precious doll's name.

It felt like a mangy cat was in the room, playing with a cornered half-dead mouse. Only Alter wasn't so sure which of the pathetic creatures he was.

'I'm not asking you to make a public confession here, Anna. I'd simply like to know the truth about your life back in Europe.' He turned to look at her. 'Who are you, Anna?'

He couldn't really blame her for keeping secrets. After all, for him secrets were the very essence of what it meant to write poetry. And most times, it was only in looking back that you realised what had been curled up inside you all along – a truth you gave birth to without ever having known it existed. And then it was there, standing before you, baring its teeth in defiance. Poetry unlocked the demons and showed him how different he was from who he saw himself to be. Yet was there a small grain of truth in anything Anna said? Or was she simply seeking safety inside an armour of deception? What nightmares were reflected off her surface sheen?

'Maybe you've mistaken me for a doll?' she said, her tone turned harsh.

Was he deliberately trying to drive her away? She decided to set him straight.

'You seem to think you can attach any narrative you want to me, Alter – accuse me of any deed. Even paint me in your likeness. That way, I will never protest, nor bear witness to your falsehood. My empty face will watch everything in silence, dreaming through painted eyes.'

Why was he so afraid to live in hope of a better world? Wasn't it his belief in the essential good in people that drove him in his quest? His hero, Don Quixote, said, 'To surrender dreams – this may be madness.' Out here, what did it matter if he was a Jew and she a German? Even the innocent child Juliet opined about her lover, Romeo, 'My only love sprung from my only hate.'

'You're right. Please forgive me,' he said, reaching out his arms to embrace her. 'My mind is turning soggy from all this rain.'

Word came through via the Overland Telegraph overnight that, weather permitting, Leaping Lena would finally be able to make it through to Birdum from Mataranka. Fergus must have been the one to slip the telegram under his door late at night. Soon, Alter would be leaving for Darwin. This, then, was to be his last day in Birdum, with Anna. What was originally meant to be a brief stay had seeped into a month. He slowly started to pack his things, carefully placing his books into the suitcase that lay open on the chair. Scraps of scrunched-up paper littered the floor – stillborn poems, wilted words. He looked across at Anna who was still asleep, breathing quietly. They had ended up spending the night together in his room, instead of hers. He folded his clothes and threw them on top of the pile of books, lifting her brassiere out from where it had fallen behind the bin. He wondered where he would be this time next week. And what of Anna?

Standing by the window, he watched the sodden ground. Grey clouds sailed across the sky. The rain had stopped. He walked over to the mirror and fastened the top button of his shirt, straightening his bow tie. He started doubting himself yet again – who could imagine a German and a Jew as lovers, anyway? Back in Europe their romance would be *verboten*. No future. And he was a man who always moved on, away from what was impossible and towards what he needed to find. He saw his face turn red. His head felt heavy, feet leaden. He should take his suitcase now and run. But where to? Anyway, he would soon be sitting in a rail carriage, watching her tiny figure grow smaller as the train pulled away from the pathetic little station, the tracks stretching ahead towards the rest of his journey.

He turned to look at Anna and found her sitting up, reading the telegraph he had left beside the bed, quietly crying. The Talmud says a man should be careful not to make a woman weep, for God will count her tears. He came and sat beside her, holding her in his arms.

'How do you make parting bearable each time you leave somewhere?' she sobbed.

Up until then they had avoided speaking of his imminent return to the city, how he would leave her behind here in Birdum. She felt fearful. His whispers, soft caresses, the warm breath on her neck; she already missed him even though he hadn't left yet. Perhaps in another city, or country, or decade, he would be hers? But out here, she would count the number of heartbeats before he disappeared on her, striding ahead, bold and full of vigour, his thoughts focused on future achievements.

For Alter, parting ways meant the hope of fresh beginnings. How to explain to her that he sought all things new, eyes forward, hoping to reach the horizon? To do so, it was essential to keep breaking away from the past. Leaving behind all that was left unsaid, silence became sandwiched between stories. He was a small explorer, one who read the future in the tea-leaves of time.

He muttered something to himself, his face taking on an earnest expression. Then the words leapt out suddenly from his mouth: 'Please come with me.'

Anna looked up at him through her tears in disbelief. 'Do you mean it?'

He smiled, sat down on the bed and took her hand. 'If you like, we can stop off to visit your Russian peanut farmers along the way. What do you say?'

She imagined packing her scant belongings into her suitcase, taking Lalka down from the shelf and wrapping her carefully in a scarf in preparation for the journey. This town had been good to her, but maybe it was finally time to move on, look for work elsewhere. She felt her drowsy mouth tingling as she answered – a trembling, sweet yes. His lips searched for her as he loosened her buttons, slipping his hand inside her blouse. They fell asleep again, entwined together like two question marks, waiting for sunrise to return their shadows to the world.

Now that the rain had stopped the shabby buildings creaked back to life, bathed in a reddish glare. Alter opened his eyes. Every inch of the landscape he had travelled through these past months was scarred by attempts at white settlement – ploughed, measured, mapped, disciplined. He and Anna were mere specks of dust against the vastness of this ancient land – two intruders searching for a home.

*

That evening she walked around the pub for the last time, a splash of light reflected onto the display of globes. The air inside was sour. Slumbering spiders lay motionless in their webs. Sometimes, Anna felt like she had been born with her eyes fixed on eternity. Instead of learning to see the here and now as a child, she had spent most of her waking moments daydreaming. She stared up at the sky, the strange light flickering above them in the heat, and tears stung her eyes. There would be no other night like this; she was already feeling a deep longing for it even though it was yet to disappear. They sat together on the veranda, surrounded by the dark blanket of evening, their bags packed, tickets ready. Leaping Lena had heaved herself into the tiny station late that afternoon and waited in the dark, ready to leave first thing in the morning. A final moment to say goodbye to Birdum, a strange place that had brought Anna love out of loss.

PART II

Eyn oyg hot mer gloybn vi tsvey oyern.
Trust one eye more than two ears.

Yiddish proverb

CHAPTER 19

MUNICH

MAY, 1915

Her left eye looked like it had been licked by some sprite hidden in the darkness of a new moon. Almost translucent, it was an icy-blue mirror in which Gustav Müller saw his own diminished reflection. But the child's right eye was olive green. She slowly drifted off to sleep as he rocked her. Fine veins crisscrossed her lids, behind which her tiny eyes flitted back and forth in wordless dreams. Holding his brand-new daughter he wept tears of love, and dread. The doctor called it heterochromia, reassuring him that famous people throughout history, the likes of Goethe and Alexander the Great, shared the anomaly. But there was also an ancient belief that a child born with different-coloured eyes was the victim of a witch replacing one eye at birth. He vowed then he would do everything in his power to protect his little girl. Those mismatched eyes could be her ticket to the world, but he feared they might also lead her straight to the grave.

There are creatures whose children float away as they are born. Gustav would keep his precious daughter near him, schooling her in literature and languages. He could already hear the taunts of horrid children, calling her a *hag's child*, preying on her other-worldly looks. Her baby heart was beating fast, her little fingers curled firmly around his thumb. The child's warm breath filled his every pore and he felt drunk on this new-found devotion. Careful not to wake her, he gently lowered her into the crib, covering her with a shawl, before tiptoeing over to the side of the bed where Ilse lay silent, her face pallid and worn. The child had drained her mother bloodless.

Bleary-eyed from lack of sleep, for a chilling moment he thought his wife was dead, but she moved her fingers slowly, beckoning him to come closer. He sat down beside her and held her hand. Several minutes passed in silence before the baby started whimpering. Lifting her from the crib, he lowered her into her mother's arms. For the first time in days, Ilse smiled.

'What shall we call her?' he asked.

'Anna,' she whispered. 'A child of grace.' Her voice sounded far away, as if she'd been swept out to sea.

CHAPTER 20

LANDSBERG

SUNDAY 6TH JULY, 1924

She was to share her toys. That's what a good girl did, Papa said. It was so kind and generous of the professor to let Anna play with the little costume dolls they collected from Fraulein Schilling's Puppetarium. Anna waited in the car one morning as the sun reached out from a sky growing warmer every day. Soon Papa was back with a new Dutch doll. They headed off, past the pastel-coloured buildings and the pretty town square where old men sat on benches around a fountain, feeding crumbs to cooing doves. They crossed the bridge, following the bends in the crystalline river as it wound its way through meadow and forest. They drove back out to the edge of town, the Alps spread across the horizon. Back at the country house, Anna raced upstairs and gently placed the Dutch doll alongside the others in her room, careful not to damage their porcelain heads. She was allowed to take some home; they were becoming part of a growing collection. The dolls came from all over the world, each one dressed in the national costume of its country. Her rarest was the Japanese Daruma doll that rested inside an ornately lacquered box. It had cranes for eyebrows, curving over blank eyes, and Fraulein Schilling explained that it was a New Year's tradition for children to paint in one of the eyes while making a wish. Last month they had brought back a Mexican doll that was apparently meant to ward off *mal de ojo*, the Evil Eye, and protect from curses that might drain your soul.

The prison was Anna's favourite building in Landsberg. With its elfin-green façade and gable roof, it looked like a castle where a princess might be trapped. Professor Jäger visited once a week, as the prison doctor. He went there to check people's eyes, but he always took along gifts for a special friend – a basket of fruit, some books and each time a different doll. Papa would pull up outside and march around the front of the car to open the door for his boss, while Anna waited in the back seat, quietly singing songs to Lalka. They usually went for a drive, or a walk together in the woods for an hour, back in time to pick up the professor when he was done.

Today, Anna sat beside the professor, clutching the new Dutch doll. She felt excited, because she had been invited to accompany him inside the green castle this time, to bring the doll to his friend herself. Just as Papa opened the door and she climbed out after the professor, holding the small Dutch doll in one hand and Lalka in the other, she heard a familiar voice.

'My dear Professor Jäger! How good to see you again.'

Anna looked up to see the same woman whom she had met in the professor's study the very first time she had been invited to Landsberg.

'Ah, Dr Magnussen. You're looking well.' The professor shook her hand eagerly.

'And I see you managed to bring our special friend along.'

'Yes.' He patted Anna on the head. 'She will be my little helper today.'

'Excellent,' she smiled. 'I am most grateful for your support.'

Anna looked around for Papa, but he was already back in the car, staring straight ahead at the road, his hands tightly gripping the steering wheel. Professor Jäger placed his hand on Anna's shoulder and guided her towards the entrance of the prison, Dr Magnussen following close behind. He signed a visitor's card, and they were led up to the second floor by a tall, greying gentleman who introduced himself as Herr Schilling, the warden.

'Our prisoner is very popular,' the elderly man said, his eyes bloodshot and pearly. 'He has entertained many, many guests since his arrival. So polite and modest. A man of such impeccable habits – he neither smokes nor drinks. It is truly a delight to have an inmate who is so well-behaved.'

'Yes, indeed. Well, let's hope he will not be staying here for the full five years of his sentence. He has much important work to do,' Dr Magnussen said, her tone sombre.

'But of course.' The warden's voice dropped to a whisper. 'I have written a report in favour of an early release. As a matter of fact, I have been making some enquiries on his behalf, regarding purchasing a car in time for that. There is a grey Benz 11/40 with wire wheels, in good condition, that I have my eye on. I am working on a discount.'

'Yes, yes. Very good.'

The man kept chatting nervously. 'I am hoping he will be out in time for the publication of his wonderful book.'

The professor silenced him with an icy stare.

The warden looked across at Anna. 'Frau . . . that is, Dr Magnussen. I must say, it is highly unusual for us to allow children inside the prison.'

'Thank you, Herr Schilling. But she is with me.' The professor stepped forward. 'Besides, I am sure you are able to make an exception,' he purred. 'You may rest assured, it is a matter of highest importance that Dr Magnussen must discuss with Herr Hitler.'

'*Natürlich*. I understand.'

The professor took the Dutch doll from Anna and handed it to the warden. 'Your daughter, the lovely Fraulein Schilling, has asked me to pass on a special gift from the Puppetarium.' He raised his eyebrows. 'I'm sure you will know just what to do with it.'

'Yes. Of course.' The warden took the doll. 'Please, follow me.'

Anna remembered Papa's words when he had handed a parcel to the dollmaker. *'And we have one to deliver as well, from your father.'* She wondered what the old warden, who had once been a dollmaker himself, was doing with all these costume dolls being ferried in and out of the prison.

'This way, please,' Herr Schilling said, leading them through an unlocked wooden door into an anteroom where a pudgy man wearing lederhosen sat with his back to them, reading a newspaper. A floral cloth covered a table laden with bowls of fruit, bottles of wine, *Leberklösse*, a plate of cakes and several boxes of chocolates. It smelled like the inside of a delicatessen. A large bouquet of flowers filled a ceramic vase.

The warden coughed loudly. 'Your visitors have arrived, *mein Führer.*'

The prisoner uncrossed his legs, adjusted his black necktie and swivelled around in his chair, surveying the group.

'Heil Hitler!' Professor Jäger stretched out his right arm in a stiff salute. 'I hope you are well, *mein Führer*. May I introduce Dr Karin Magnussen, whose fascinating research we have already discussed at length?'

The woman shuffled forward awkwardly. 'Heil Hitler!' she saluted. 'An honour to meet you, sir,' she added in a fawning tone.

The prisoner reached out and took a bite of torte, leaving a dollop of cream hanging from his tiny moustache. 'I will forever be indebted to our dear Professor Jäger here, who helped me recover from my injury during the war.'

Anna bit the inside of her cheek, trying not to giggle as she watched the cream bob up and down while the man spoke.

'Back in 1918, when I was a mere corporal, I was caught in a ghastly mustard-gas attack by the British. I spent the rest of the war in a military hospital, suffering from total blindness.'

Dr Magnussen brought her hand up to her throat. Professor Jäger had indeed told her about this interesting case, which had been treated as hysterical amblyopia, a psychiatric disorder, described as a flight from reality into illness. She had read some interesting papers published, in which patients who believed they were blind were proven to have normal vision on optometric testing.

'Is that so? That must have been so terrible for you,' she said. 'He has never mentioned this to me.' She noticed the man raise his eyebrows and, glancing at her colleague, quickly added: 'But that would only be because he is highly cautious about maintaining patient confidentiality.'

'I was fortunate to have him as my neighbour in Munich,' the prisoner continued. 'He led the excellent team of doctors who helped save my sight. I know what it is to lie for months on end, unable to see. But you know, it was during those very hours of darkness my true vision came to me – that I would liberate Germany, that I would make it great.' He pointed to some notebooks stacked up on a sideboard. 'In fact, I am dictating my memoir to Herr Hess here,

my dear colleague and loyal companion in our struggle to restore
Germany to its former glory.'

A man with dark bushy eyebrows rose from his chair and bowed
formally.

'Dr Magnussen. It is my pleasure to introduce you to my dear
colleague, Herr Rudolf Hess. He was there with me when we
marched in Munich last November. I dislocated my shoulder in
that skirmish, you know, but I could have easily died, if it wasn't
for my brave bodyguard shielding me from the bullets. And the
cheek of them to charge me with treason, when all we were trying
to do is save our country from the so-called democracy of the
Jewish Weimar Republic, and other unsavoury criminal elements.
Rudolf has kindly agreed to transcribe everything into a little book
I hope to have published as soon as I am out of here. Professor Jäger
is kindly helping us with this matter. To think they would try to
ban my work!'

'That is precisely why Professor Jäger has asked me to come here
to talk to you today.' Karin Magnussen seized the opportunity to
direct the discussion towards her work. 'This is the young girl he
was telling you about, *mein Führer*.'

'Bring her to me.'

Dr Magnussen placed her hand on Anna's back and urged her
closer. Anna didn't move.

'Go on. Don't be shy, child,' she said, nudging Anna forward.

Anna stared at the floor, the room beginning to spin. She felt
one of her nerve storms coming on, her heart racing.

The man called Hitler reached across and lifted her chin. She
could not avoid his icy-blue eyes staring at her with a fierce intensity that made her squeamish.

'You see each one is a different colour, *mein Führer*?'

'Fascinating,' He squinted, as though he were examining some rare gemstone. 'The left one is a perfect blue; *Himmelfarb*, the colour of a brilliant sky.' He turned Anna's head to the left. 'And yet the other is murky green, like a Jew.'

'Precisely, *mein Führer*. This is a genetic condition called heterochromia iridis.' Dr Magnussen pulled out some charts from her briefcase. 'If you will permit me to show you.' She spread them out on the tablecloth. 'My colleague Dr Karl Saller, a well-respected anthropologist, has designed a revolutionary new way to determine racial hygiene by scientifically assessing the whiteness of mixed-race people according to the colour of their irises. My own research – called *The Eye Colour Experiment* – goes a step further. I have found that injecting adrenaline into the eyes of rabbits can turn their irises blue. This could revolutionise our cause of Aryanisation, with the proper funding of course. Imagine the impact if we were able to perform trials on human subjects. There is a group of Sinti, many of whom I believe have heterochromia. They would make a perfect case study.'

'Hmm. Interesting. I shall speak to my good friend Alfred Rosenberg next time he comes to visit. I have appointed him the leader of our movement during my stay here. He is an interest-ing fellow, who is himself building the theory of a racial ladder, with what he refers to as *Untermenschen* on the bottom rung and Aryans like us at the top. He is particularly interested in the Jewish Question.' He reached across and picked up a book resting on the table. 'You should read this. *Immorality in the Talmud*. Rosenberg wrote it. I can lend it to you, if you like. Of course, the criminals have banned our party, but we are still finding all sorts of creative ways of communicating beyond these walls, as you well know.'

Hitler smiled at Anna. He turned towards a blond man who was strumming a mandolin: 'Emill. Put that thing down, will you, and come meet our esteemed guest. And why don't you invite your delicious friend over there to join us for some tea and Linzer torte.'

A woman smoking a cigarette emerged from behind a screen. She avoided Anna's eyes as she sat down at the table. It was the Lady of the Flowery Dresses – Tantine.

CHAPTER 21

KATHERINE

SATURDAY 22ND OCTOBER, 1938

As they stepped off the train mid-afternoon they were greeted by a goat, bleating insistently as it wagged its tail. A thick cord was tied around its scraggy neck, the frayed end dragging in the mud. The heat was stifling. Alter sighed. Anna squeezed his hand. She had encouraged a stopover in Katherine so that he might see the sense of community among some of the immigrants she had met over the years.

The goat started butting its head against Alter's suitcase, as if it recognised an old friend. Alter grabbed the rope and the animal licked his trouser leg as it followed them towards the stationmaster's office, a whitewashed wooden building with a long veranda and a corrugated-iron roof. A lonely cloud scudded slowly across the horizon, haloes of flies and mosquitoes buzzed around them. Anna's stomach rumbled. She felt a sudden urge for a serving of fried fish, even though they were 200 miles away from the nearest ocean.

A group of children rushed towards them, shouting excitedly. One young boy with fair hair and freckles made a beeline for the goat.

'Pirozhki! *Idi syuda!*' He stood in front of them, holding out his hand to entice the goat to come to him.

Handing over the rope, with Pirozhki attached, Alter bent down to whisper something in the boy's ear.

'*Spasiba,*' the child answered in perfect Russian, then doffed his hat and bowed to Anna. 'Thank you,' he said, with an equally distinctive Australian twang.

Alter embarked on an animated discussion with the boy. They spoke in Russian like two long-lost friends, smiling as they took turns to pat the goat on its head. Words flew between them like flapping birds, Alter's voice quavering with enthusiasm.

He turned to Anna. 'Truth lies with children and fools.'

She smiled but didn't bother questioning what he meant. He might be a poet, but sometimes he spoke in such cryptic riddles that she found it a little tiresome. She looked out beyond the station, towards the town. Compared to Birdum it was a bustling metropolis.

As they walked slowly away from the station, the boy and his goat followed close behind.

'Who would believe it?' Alter said. 'A child speaking Russian, right here at the edge of the world.'

He stopped suddenly in front of a sign posted on a hut, as though he had been struck by lightning, reading the bold Cyrillic script out loud. There was an English translation scribbled underneath:

Administrative Office
Russian Peanut Farmers Association
Katherine

'*Pyotr!*' A man wearing jodhpurs tucked into high leather boots came running towards them.

He wore a fleece *papakha* on his head, a type of hat Alter had seen worn by Cossacks back in Russia. The fingers of the man's left hand were latched inside the top of a brightly coloured waistcoat. He spoke sternly in Russian to the boy, pointing towards a crowd of people in the distance. Turning away, the child tugged on the rope and retreated, followed reluctantly by the goat.

The man held his hands out to Anna. 'Hello, my dear. Good to see you again after so long.' It had been two years since he had visited Birdum. He gently touched his lips to the back of Anna's hand, and then turned to Alter.

'Jack,' he said, holding out his hand as he bowed. 'My apologies to you both. They grow up a little too wild around here, I'm afraid.'

Alter liked a man with a firm handshake. 'I am Alter Mayseh. And I think he's a lovely boy.'

'Ha ha! I meant the goat. She's a reckless, foolish thing. But her milk is as sweet as manna from Heaven.' Jack smiled at Anna, and turned back to Alter. 'My late wife was the visiting doctor for the area, until she herself took ill and died a few months later.'

'I'm so very sorry to hear that.' Alter looked down at his feet.

The urgent whistling of a bird pierced the awkward silence.

'Ah, well,' Jack said. 'Sadly, that is God's will. But at least her memory is carried by our young Pyotr. She would have wanted us to live our lives to the fullest.' Jack slapped the side of his thigh and beamed at them. 'So, you were stuck in Birdum because of the rains?'

Alter glanced at Anna. 'Not for too long.'

'Well then, welcome to Katherine. Come! Let me show you around our lovely township. I insist that you stay with me.'

'That's very kind of you, um, Jack.' Alter looked at him quizzic-ally. 'If I may be so bold, what is your Russian name?'

The tall man laughed. '*Da, da, da!* Yes, of course. My name is Arkady Ivanov, but here everyone calls me Jack.'

A few ramshackle houses were huddled together along one side of the river. Jack carried their bags in one hand. He was tall and broad-shouldered, with bushy eyebrows shading his blue-grey eyes. Alter followed him towards the main street. Anna walked beside him, imagining she caught the scent of cinnamon in the air. Jack led them along a route past the ruins of an old shack. The sound of a mandolin came from inside. A sweet melody.

'That is Oleg, playing his *bandura*,' Jack said. 'You have arrived at the perfect time. Today is a festive day for us. The celebration of our annual peanut harvest.'

They reached a crowd of people, all in their finest Cossack dress. The women wore traditional red frocks with colourful ribbons and scarves threaded through their hair. A young girl sang like a nightingale as she stood beside a wild pig roasting on a spit. They all congregated in front of a shack with a makeshift cross tied to its roof – a school doubling as a church. It nestled between a pub and a post office. There was plenty of laughter and an abundance of vodka.

From the other end of the dusty main street, a black horse came galloping towards them. A man stood on its back, jumping up and turning to land in the saddle backwards. He was followed by three more horses, straddled by a team of acrobats performing somer-saults and handstands as they hurtled past the cheering crowd.

Anna dropped her hat. Out of the blue, a young rider holding a whip between his teeth came racing up on his horse and, with a spectacular leap, picked the hat up and placed it back on her head. Before she knew it, he had remounted and galloped off down the main street.

Jack laughed. 'Cossacks have always been excellent horsemen, and these tricks have given us the reputation of being unconquerable. It is called *dzhigitovka*,' he said. 'It turns the rider into a deadly strike weapon. Even Napoleon said with just the Cossacks alone, he could conquer all of Europe.'

The indigo sky was turning dark. Jack invited them to join him for tea, which ended up being accompanied by a few too many shots of vodka for them all. The lives of forgotten people hung heavy in the air, voices of writers, poets and musicians from far away, echoing the past. Alter told him how he had made his way to Warsaw as a young man, joining the Haliastra, a group of artists and writers who were filled with dreams of a new world. Galloping Jack, it turned out, had turned his misfortune into song. A gifted violinist and painter, he fled from the freshly formed Communist regime and frozen tundras of Russia.

'Music was my passport out of there,' Jack told them. 'My family came from Yekaterinburg. When the Whites and Reds converged on the Urals, my parents packed all they could into a wooden box and two large suitcases and piled us onto the roof of a crowded train headed to Omsk. I kept my violin beside me the whole way across Siberia.' He stroked the case of his violin. 'After several weeks we reached Manchuria, and soon settled into our new life, in Harbin. My mother called it the Moscow of the East.'

Talking about the destruction of their former lives sobered the two men a little. Alter looked around Jack's shanty. Tins of beans and sardines were piled up against one wall.

'I won't eat anything fresh,' Jack confessed. He pointed to a pile of empty tins in a basket in the corner. 'Although, if Communist spies decide to come all the way over here to poison me, it would be a far better fate than being taken back to Russia, I suppose.'

He and his young son lived in a hut with a makeshift roof of corrugated iron, their beds formed from compacted ant mounds. Alter could see the mark of how high the waters had reached when the river overflowed its bank. An old truck stood out back. Jack led his visitors across the yard towards it. He invited them in, helping Anna step up some rickety stairs and through a doorway at the side. She rubbed her eyes in disbelief. It looked like a robber's hideout filled with shiny jewels, a secret cave of forgotten treasures.

Strings of silvery planets ran from floor to ceiling. They were fashioned from empty sardine tins. Jack had built a universe in the back of his truck, with tin galaxies clinking in the gentle breeze. Painted comets twirled about on chains. Much of the wire ceiling had caved in under its astronomical weight and the iron sun had been corroded by weather. A sign painted in giant childish script shouted: *PLANETARIUM*.

The pale hem of day started fraying. A chorus of cicadas trilled as night surrounded them. Anna looked up at the moon between the wires and couldn't be sure if it was real, or part of Jack's sculpted world. In the distance, a nightbird howled like a mother who had lost her child. Along one side the roof was open to the fading sky. Above the other side, it was already night and stars winked at them. It smelled of rust and dust. And something else, too – the whiff of rotting fish.

Jack stood up, a little wobbly on his feet. 'A toast to this country that has given us shelter. Thank you for visiting us, Anna and Alter. Here's to your onward journey, my friends. *Prost!*'

Alter raised his glass. 'Here's to a better world.'

Anna peered through the chicken-wire roof at the rain clouds gathering again above them. 'I'll drink to that!'

CHAPTER 22

MUNICH

FEBRUARY, 1933

When Anna got home from school, dirty dishes were still piled up in the sink. She rinsed them before preparing dinner.

Afterwards she stood in front of the mirror, pulling her hair out of a ponytail, letting the long strands fall around her shoulders. A child no longer stared back at her. She had grown into a woman's body, a stranger taking over both her heart and mind. It was getting late. Anna had been waiting for Papa to return. While fog descended on the city their dinner had turned cold, the smell of sauerkraut and sausage hanging in the kitchen. In one corner of Papa's room stood a leather suitcase. She had noticed it lying open when she arrived home, some of Papa's clothes shoved inside. Papers were scattered across his desk, the drawers pulled out, as though he had been searching for something. He must have come home early and left again. But why was he packing?

Suddenly she heard the familiar sound of a Mercedes pull up out front, and rushed to the bedroom window. Looking down, she saw Professor Jäger step out of the car, but it wasn't Papa who had run around from the driver's seat to open the door for him. Instead, there was a young man with blond hair, dressed in a different uniform, wearing an armband emblazoned with a swastika. Anna hurried to tidy Papa's desk as she heard Professor Jäger make his way up the wooden staircase and waited for a knock on the front door.

'Good evening, my dear.' He took off his hat as she opened the door, sweeping his hand through his greasy hair as he smoothed it away from his eyes. He stood in the stairwell staring at her.

'Papa isn't home yet,' Anna said.

'Oh, but I'm here to see you, my dearest.' He laughed as he waited to be invited in. 'How is my little collector?'

Anna shifted from one foot to the other. 'I'm well, thank you, Herr Professor.'

'And I hear you are finishing your studies soon?'

'Yes, sir.' She stepped aside as he edged his way past her.

'Good, good.' He headed straight towards the sofa. 'That is excellent.'

Without taking off his coat he sat down and patted the cushion beside him, inviting her to join him. On the wall beside them hung a family photograph of Anna as a toddler, seated on her mother's lap, Papa resting his fingertips on the back of the chair as he stared proudly into the camera lens.

'It's been a while since you came to visit us in Landsberg, hasn't it?'

'Yes, Herr Professor.'

'Such a pity. I do miss having young people around to keep me company. Why don't you come and stay for a few days?'

'Thank you kindly, but I like to spend most of my free time here with Papa.'

'Indeed. But that's why I popped in. You see, your father had to go away, *meine Schönheit*. Important business.'

My beauty? He had never used such a syrupy tone with her before.

'In fact, he has asked me to take care of you while he is gone. I wanted to let you know in person that Hans will pick you up at noon tomorrow and drive you straight to Landsberg, where you will be staying with me for a while. You are to pack some clothes and a few personal effects.' He sneezed loudly into his hand-kerchief, peering at her over his spectacles, his eyes bloodshot and watery.

Why had Papa not mentioned any of this to her? She tried to sound calm, hesitating before asking: 'How long will he be away?'

'Well, that depends, my dear,' he said quietly. 'You have grown into a very beautiful and intelligent young woman, and no doubt you must be feeling so excited by all the changes taking place in our wonderful Fatherland of late. You are in your final year of school now, am I correct?' He didn't wait for an answer. 'I'm sure you are learning fascinating things in your studies of race science and geopolitics.' His voice became shrill, as though he were deliv-ering a carefully rehearsed speech to a large audience. 'There is so much that our youth can contribute to the cause. And I have come here today because I have something very special to ask of you, which will give you the opportunity to show us your true dedication.'

She felt her heart pounding against her chest.

The professor continued. 'I would hate to feel humiliated by any betrayal of the trust I have placed in you. We have known each other since you were a little girl, and I can assure you no harm will come to you.'

She bit her lip, trying to stifle her tears.

'Don't get so worked up, my dear. I would hate you to get one of your dreadful migraines, or nerve storms as your silly father called them. Your dear Papa will be safe too – that is, if you agree to volunteer your service to the party.' He reached out and held her chin firmly in his hand. 'Those eyes of yours really are quite fascinating, aren't they?'

She stayed perfectly still, trying not to gag from the acrid smell of his breath. 'What is it that you would you like me to do, professor?'

'Ah, well. We must all contribute in our own way, and I am asking you to play your part in building the Fatherland, bringing Germany back to its former glory.' He let go of her. His face looked carved from stone. 'You will remember our dear friend Dr Magnussen, of course?'

How could she forget this woman, who had visited her nightmares ever since they met for the first time?

He leaned forward. 'Well, I would like you to help her with some very important research. Those peculiar eyes of yours could contribute so much to our understanding of racial genetics. If we can find the key to eye colour we can build a *Volk* of true, blue-eyed Aryan beauty.'

The clock went on ticking, but Anna felt time stand still as the reality of what the professor was asking her to do sank in. She remembered the tiny rabbits huddled together in their hutch at Landsberg all those years ago, their eyes reddened and scarred. And she could still feel her visceral horror upon learning what Dr Magnussen did to the poor creatures' eyeballs in her experiments, injecting adrenaline into them to try to turn them blue.

'I'm sure you would do anything for your dear, misguided papa. I would hate to see him come to harm because his daughter has decided to become a little wayward herself. We wouldn't want anything bad to happen to him now, would we?'

His threat plunged like a needle into her heart. She glanced out the window at the steel evening descending on the town. Suddenly rising from the sofa, the professor made his way towards the front door.

'Well, I'd better be on my way. It's getting late.' He stood there waiting for her to see him out. 'Good night, dearest Anna. I very much look forward to seeing you in Landsberg tomorrow afternoon.'

'Good night, Professor Jäger.' Closing the door behind him, she pressed her hands against the lock, feeling like she had fallen into a gaping chasm.

She ran to Papa's desk. Rummaging through a small pile of papers sitting on top, she found an envelope with her name scribbled on it. Her hands shook as she pulled out a wad of money, the notes fluttering to the floor. She unfolded a piece of paper that listed all her personal details. In the top corner Papa had scrawled a short message:

> You are in great danger, Anna. They are coming. Don't trust Jäger! Find Shmontz in Pinocchio and give him this. Save yourself. I am sorry.

She glanced at the family photo. All of them were smiling as they looked forward, not knowing how the rest of their lives would unfold. As she stared at Papa's eyes, she remembered his trembling voice one evening as he sat beside her on the sofa.

'Your mother was the kindest soul I ever knew. She always tried to help everyone as much as she could, no matter how poor they were or which God they worshipped. She also loved you very much, and I only wish she could be here to see what a wonderful woman you have become. I know she would have been so proud of you. But Anna, not everyone is like your mother; there are good people and bad people in this world. Germany is changing, my darling and it is becoming harder and harder to know who you can trust nowadays. This country is no longer the place your mutti loved so much.'

She ran to the bookshelf in her room and pulled out the book she had treasured as a child, with its fine gold lettering and the drawing of a skinny little puppet with a long, wooden nose and funny hat. It had been years since she had read it. Opening the cover, she found an address in Papa's handwriting tucked inside. Tearing out the page, she placed it hastily in the pocket of her dress. She had to find the man they called Shmontz.

CHAPTER 23

KATHERINE GORGE

SUNDAY 23RD OCTOBER, 1938

Alter cautiously lowered himself into the hot springs while Anna stripped off her dress and ran down to the bank, disappearing underwater with a gentle splash. How deep was it, he wondered? He searched for bubbles to track her. She soon surfaced like a water nymph and swam towards him.

'Where did you learn to swim like that?'

'I used to visit the countryside often with my father. There was a beautiful river there where I spent many a lazy summer afternoon as a child.'

They stood together near the edge, the stars reflected in the water. The moon sliced the night sky like a sliver of bone, avulsed from the earth. They searched for Pegasus, Cancer and Corvus, but the stars were strangers here, painting a different narrative suspended above them, a net of ancient stories lighting up the darkness. She had always loved to create her own constellations, tattooed onto an inky canvas – a giant with flowing white hair stomping across the heavens, a young girl playing in a bathtub, sending a splash of watery planets spilling onto the celestial vista.

'They are like eyes, watching us.' Alter made a pillow for his head with his palms. 'An empyrean audience for a man who appeared out of nowhere.'

Anna longed for a love as steady as the stars.

He turned to her. 'This is not our place.'

'But neither is Europe anymore,' she whispered.

'So where do we belong then? Where should we call home?'

'Here.' She placed her palm on his chest. 'Remember? This is home.'

Frogs floated around, bobbing their heads up before kicking away, leaving ripples behind them. Tall eucalypts stood silhouetted against the last jagged rays of light.

A huge colony of fruit bats slowly awoke, hanging upside down in the trees, busily preening their wings in readiness for flight. They looked like small teddy bears with black beady eyes, hanging upside down on a rack, silken capes hiding their furry breasts. Their cries rose to a frenzied crescendo as they launched themselves into the air, darting from branch to branch. Anna watched mother bats trying to pry themselves away from their babies, who clung steadfastly to their breasts, drunk with sleep. Some left young ones behind in a nursery tree, huddling together in a tangle of commotion, but others took flight, launching their bodies into the gentle night breeze, their tiny offspring refusing to let go.

The calls of the waking colony echoed against the darkening cliff faces. The bats set out to forage for food just as flocks of black cockatoos were making their way home to roost. More bats emerged from the trees in a flurry of beating wings. They rose in widening circles, forming shadowy clouds that seemed to share a single heartbeat.

Their cacophony highlighted the silence that lingered between Anna and Alter. She felt embarrassed by her silly romantic hopes which, in the end, might only amount to no more than a fleeting blink. She rehearsed words to herself before uttering them, fearful they might come out wrong. Thoughts shaped themselves into storm clouds in her mind, evaporating into mist as she tried to mould them into logical sentences. Besides, what was there to say? The ghastly contorted messiness of *I love you*, or *be mine*, terrified her.

Alter broke the silence. 'You know, three of the most prominent biblical figures – Isaac, Jacob and Moses – met their wives for the first time beside a well. Don't you think that's a portent?'

She looked at him blankly.

He smiled. 'I mean, that is, like you and me. We met on top of a water tower. That's surely the modern-day equivalent of a well?'

She giggled nervously, glad he couldn't see her blushing. 'Why won't you go in deeper?'

'I'm embarrassed to admit I'm a poor swimmer,' he whispered. 'According to an ancient Jewish tradition it is a father's duty to teach his son to swim, but mine didn't know how.'

'What about daughters? Are they taught as well?'

'Well, you see, that's the problem. A lake is formed from the teardrops of little girls. So they would drown in their own sadness if they tried to swim.'

'That's a terrifying thought.'

'Jews have a complicated relationship with bodies of water. At New Year we are meant to throw bread into a lake, a symbolic way to cast away sins. It's called *tashlikh* – a prayer for repentance.'

'But then if you went swimming in the same spot soon after, wouldn't you just swallow your sins all over again?'

'That's an interesting thought.' He scratched his beard. 'You're supposed to throw your sins where there are fish in the water, so they can swallow them for you.' He reached up to his bag and pulled out a half-eaten, stale loaf of bread he had brought all the way from Birdum. 'Because my father couldn't swim and was so terrified I might drown when I was a boy, we used to do *tashlikh* in the courtyard of our apartment building. He used a bucket of water instead of a lake.'

Alter tore pieces off the loaf and threw them into the springs, chanting a prayer in Hebrew.

'Stop!'

'What's wrong, Anna?'

'I don't want the fish to swallow our sins. They haven't done anything wrong.'

'Don't worry. New year has finished, so we have another year to repent. Besides, they don't have eyelids.'

'What's that got to do with anything?'

'A fish's eyes are always open, so they aren't vulnerable to the Evil Eye like humans are. Fish are always watching, just as God is supposed to be watching over us.'

She thought for a moment. 'But fish can be caught in a fisherman's net.'

'That's true. But we too are caught in the net of judgement. Besides, fish have many offspring, so there is always hope in a new generation.'

He took a penknife from his pocket and sliced an apple Jack had given him, stabbing a piece and offering it to Anna. She leaned forward and gripped it between her teeth, sliding it off the sharp metal.

'I have so many stories. I'm thinking of writing a memoir,' he said. 'After all, I've lived a life of adventure enough for a hundred men. Perhaps I will call it *Der Maysehbuch fun Meyn Leben.*' He snorted. 'Ha! Alter Mayseh's *maysehbuch.*'

Anna looked up at the sky.

'Don't you get it?'

'No.'

'Mayseh is my name. It means "story" in Yiddish. So, a *maysehbuch* is the storybook of my life.'

She still didn't see what was so amusing.

'*Ach!* It's impossible to translate Yiddish humour.' He laughed.

'Clearly.'

He looked up at her. She wasn't smiling.

'Are you upset?'

Against her better judgement, she launched her accusation like an arrow: 'Am I just one of your side adventures, to be had while you catch your breath? Your little *shikseh* on the side before you find a Jewish bride?'

'Is that really what you think of me?' As he got out of the water, Alter hit his head against the sharp edge of a branch that was jutting out. In an instant, his legs buckled and he collapsed. He mumbled something, a half-smile crossing his lips, and fell into a sweaty stupor. She swam across and hauled herself onto the bank. His eyes were darting around frantically under closed lids. The cut on his forehead started oozing, spreading to form a bloody stain on his wet undershirt. She pulled a handkerchief from her bag and dabbed at the wound. She would have to go and find help, leave him here alone under the cover of drooping eucalypts.

'You're bleeding, Alter. I'm going to look for some help. Please don't move.' She quickly put her on clothes. 'I'll be back as soon as I can.'

He didn't reply. Propping him up on a bed of leaves, she covered him with his shirt and headed off into the scrub. She stepped into the night, leaving Alter in almost total darkness, the only meagre light coming from the scimitar moon. She was struck with terror at the real possibility that he would die because she would not be able to find her way back to him. The bats shrieked, a cool breeze whispering between the rocks. She tore small strips of material from her hem, hanging them off branches every few hundred metres as she walked. Despite all attempts, it wasn't long before her fear collided with reality as she wandered around in the dark, completely lost. The paralysing heat of the sun had given way to piercing cold. She was feeling tired and shivery, almost ready to give up, when she stumbled across a lonely grave surrounded by a wooden picket fence. Behind it stood a run-down old shack. At first glance, the house looked abandoned, but a figure soon emerged from the shadows, eerily lit up by a sputtering kerosene lamp. She missed the dead, but now certainly wasn't a time that she wanted them to come back and haunt her.

The ghost didn't look too ghoulish, and it had a broad Australian drawl. 'You all right there?'

'I'm lost.'

'Well, that's pretty damn obvious, love.'

Even though she felt wary coming across a stranger living alone out here in the middle of the bush, she had no choice but to trust him.

'I must get back to the springs. My friend has hit his head. Would you please help me, sir?'

'Sir? Ha! Never been called that before. Takes a bloody foreigner to be so polite. Yeah. Gimme a minute, I'll go get us a decent lamp.'

Leaving Anna waiting in the dark, he went inside the shack again. He was back soon, a strong circle of light swinging beside him.

She followed close behind as they made their way through thickets and trees.

'Why the hell were you both wandering around here at night? Not the cleverest thing to do.'

'A man called Jack suggested it. Said these springs are so powerful they can even heal a broken heart.'

'You mean the Russian bloke?'

'Yes.'

'I wouldn't listen to that fellow if ya paid me. Goes off like a frog in a sock.'

'It's my fault, really. I didn't realise it was getting so late.'

'Not that hard to lose track of time out here.'

'Do you live in that house?'

'Yeah. The locals call it the Ghost House. Reckon someone who was murdered nearby years ago haunts the place. But the only spirit you'll ever see around these parts is this one right here.' He raised the bottle of rum he was holding. 'Cheers!'

Suddenly, Anna caught sight of one of the torn pieces of her dress hanging from a branch. 'He's somewhere around here!'

Just then she heard Alter groaning. They found him lying in the same place she had left him, by the edge of the springs.

'Here, hold this.' The Ghost Man handed both his lantern and the bottle of rum to Anna.

Pulling an old bandage from his pocket, he tied it around Alter's head, then lifted him up onto his back like a sack of potatoes. Anna gathered up his clothes. 'Walk in front of me and I'll tell you which way to head.'

It took some time, beating their way through the bush, but they eventually made it back to the old shack. Ghost Man placed Alter onto a thin mattress that lay on a rusty bed frame and covered him with a blanket. He removed the tattered bandage from Alter's head, poured some rum from the half-empty bottle onto it and dabbed it onto the wound.

'*Ribono shel oylem!*' Alter sat bolt upright. 'Lord of the Universe! Where am I?'

'Well, that worked a treat,' Ghost Man muttered. 'Here, give him a swig of this.' He handed the bottle to Anna.

Gently supporting the back of Alter's head, she brought the bottle to his lips.

'Have a drink, darling. You fell and hit your head. This kind man helped me carry you back to his house.'

Alter's eyes were swollen, and the cut on his forehead was ringed by large welts. He downed the rum eagerly and immediately fell asleep again.

'How long do you reckon he was out for?' Ghost Man mumbled.

'It all happened so quickly, I'm not quite sure.'

'Well, you should watch him closely overnight. Grab a blanket and make yourself comfortable.' He stretched his arms out and yawned. 'I'm gonna try get some kip.'

Anna sat cross-legged on the floor beside the bed, keeping vigil, while Ghost Man crawled off to sleep in a broken armchair.

Alter had been drifting in and out of a state of torpor for hours when light poured in through the faded curtains. The hut felt stifling, ablaze with scraps of leftover dreams that hung in the smouldering air, evaporating the moment he woke. He got up and staggered across the room, tearing open the window and shutters. A rush of heat from the first rays of sun forced its way inside. Overcome with vertigo, he lay back down again, listening to the melancholy sound of a clock somewhere close by, ticking away each second. The mattress was drenched in sweat and streaked with blood. He felt tired and worn, his head throbbing as he uttered wordless curses. He burrowed his face in the hard pillow.

Signs of Anna were scattered about the room. Like a tiny bird, she had been flitting to and fro all night, watching him, and had finally succumbed to sleep, sprawled out on the dusty floor. He felt weak, the shrieking of crickets outside drilling into his brain. Lying there watching her through half-closed eyes, he curled back into the refuge of sleep.

Ghost Man had disappeared.

PART III

A tropn libe brengt a mol a yam trern.
A drop of love can bring an ocean of tears.

Yiddish proverb

CHAPTER 24

MELBOURNE

TUESDAY 6ᵀᴴ DECEMBER, 1938

Anna stretched out on the blanket, digging her toes in the sand. They had caught the tram across town from Carlton all the way to St Kilda Beach, just to cool off from the heat. Along the way, Anna had looked wistfully at Christmas decorations glittering in shop windows. Alter was the guest of a local Jewish family, the Eisners, who put him up in their home in the suburb of Brunswick. He eked out a meagre living by writing articles for the *Australian Jewish Herald*. Meanwhile, Anna was living nearby, in a bungalow out back of an elderly widow's house, earning a small stipend for helping with meals and chores. Both Alter and Anna loved spending weekends together, exploring their new city.

Alter sat beside her, staring silently out to sea, his notebook abandoned beside him. Yawning loudly, he stood up and raised his arms above his head. 'I'm going to take a dip.'

'Don't go in too deep, Alter.'

'You don't have to remind me I can't swim, Anna.'

He made his way down to the water's edge and waded slowly in the shallows alongside the wooden pier. Anna followed him, picking her way gingerly over mounds of broken shells, till she reached the shoreline. White sails ballooned on the horizon, fat-bellied gulls shrieking as they circled overhead. A pelican stared at her, sunning itself on a rock nearby. A hoard of sandflies congregated around a bloated jellyfish. Her feet were swallowed by the foam and froth of the waves, ribbons of kelp washing up beside her. Empty abalone shells glistened like jewels in the sand alongside mussels, limpets and the carapaces of crabs hidden among the rotting seaweed. Dumped onto the beach by waves, they lay abandoned by a receding tide. Just like her and Alter, she thought – washed up on a distant shore by the vagaries of history and time, parched and shrivelled under a harsh sun. She ran back to the safety of the picnic blanket.

She sat down again, squinting as she watched Alter. Should she be worried that he might be out of his depth, alert the lifeguards, those strong Australian men with broad smiles and broad chests? But he was already making his way slowly towards shore.

A sudden gust of wind blew open Alter's notebook, tickling it with feathery fingers that seemed to beckon her to peer into his most private thoughts. She pinned down the pages, stealing a glimpse at the words he kept secret from her. Sentences burst into distorted shapes, sprawling along the lines. She should have realised he still hid his life behind the hieroglyphics of a tongue so foreign to her eyes that it resembled the whorls and spirals of the waves. She wondered what she had been expecting to find – fluent German sonnets penned in perfect *Sütterlin*, or poetry written with English cursive loops? She already knew he wrote in Yiddish.

The rhythmic sound of the waves lapping against the shore soothed her. Alter was wading back, lurching awkwardly from side to side. He ran up to her and shook himself like a wet puppy. The salty droplets cooled her skin. He dived onto the blanket beside her and gave her a sodden hug.

'Stop it!' she squealed.

A shaggy brown dog rushed up to them, its tail thrashing like a propellor.

'Shoo!' Alter tried to chase it away, but it darted to and fro, sniffing for food before its owner whistled for it to come.

The gulls circled. One brave bird sat down next to them, folding its red spindly legs under its belly. Its grey feathers ruffled in the breeze as it warmed itself on a bed of sand, watching them intently. Anna threw it a crust of bread. The bird dived on it, hastily flying away before being chased by other gulls. The sun was hot, but as the afternoon wore on the breeze whipped up.

They packed up their things and made their way back towards St Kilda's Village Belle, strolling past Luna Park, the gaping plaster face of Mr Moon trying to swallow them into his maws. The Scenic Railway jostled people up and down, their screams reaching out across the bay. They finished off a pleasant afternoon with *Kugelhopf* and Polish cheesecake from Monarch Cakes on Acland Street, as delicious as you might find in any *Konditorei* back home. She liked Melbourne. It felt so familiar in many ways, a city with a truly distinctive European flavour.

That evening, crowds gathered to celebrate Alter's arrival back in Melbourne. He had been invited to give a lecture at the Kadimah, the Jewish cultural centre in Carlton. The hall was filled with people eager to hear his lecture about *The Dybbuk*, a play by Ansky originally written in Russian but later translated into Yiddish.

The newly released film was to be screened for the first time on Australian shores shortly, to everyone's immense excitement. Alter mounted the stage, all eyes raised towards him. The audience was seated in rows inside the dim hall, but he could still make out the rapture in expectant faces. To those present he was a famous Yiddish poet bringing a taste of home and of the lives they had left behind in Europe. Here in Melbourne, where they had been given a chance to start afresh, they were trying to rebuild a world of secular Yiddish that had occupied the core of their existence. Alter lapped up the attention despite knowing his celebrity was over-inflated, but it felt flattering nonetheless. They seemed to hang on every word he had to say.

'An immigrant is like a *dybbuk*,' he said, going straight for the jugular, 'a dislocated soul, searching for a body to possess. We are all *dybbuks* of a sort – Jewish wanderers forced to straddle the world of the *shtetl* left behind and the newness of a city with forty-eight Albert Streets. We each weave our old-world sensibilities with this new landscape. I want to help recreate our vanished world – not to blend in, but to transplant an entire culture through theatre, education, literary works and a flourishing press. Let's make Yiddish the language of our everyday lives, alongside the King's English; a secular identity, divorced from the rituals of prayer and devotion. Not adaptation and assimilation, but instead embracing a vibrant culture that already exists. Cliques, schisms, fractures, complexity, passionate dissent and debate – where there is one Jew, you have one opinion. But where there are many Jews, there are many arguments.'

He was met with rapturous applause and was excited to find such a vibrant and enthusiastic Yiddish-speaking commu-nity. Afterwards, people waited to meet him and shake his hand. A short, balding man who had been busily stacking up the folding chairs hovered at the back like a tattered moth. It was only when the crowd had started to disperse and Alter was packing his papers into his leather satchel, preparing to leave, that the fellow stepped forward. He cleared his throat to get Alter's attention. With edgy distraction, Alter looked up. He was greeted by a broad, enthusiastic grin, which he returned with a tolerant smile.

'Retter,' the man held out his hand. 'Leo Retter. Do you remember me?'

Alter's smile melted from his face. Clearly not.

'We met at Station Pier, on the very day you arrived.'

'Ah, yes! Of course.' Alter had no recollection at all of this man and turned to introduce him to Anna, in the hope that he might give her some sort of a clue.

'This is my dear friend Miss Anna Winter. I found her in the middle of the desert, would you believe?'

Leo bowed, kissing the back of her hand. 'A pleasure to meet you. Any friend of Alter's is a friend of mine.'

'That's very kind of you, Mr Retter.' Anna had caught Alter's wink and understood he needed rescuing. 'How exactly do you two know each other?'

'Oh! My dear, late uncle was an ardent fan of Mr Mayseh's work in the *Literarische Bleter*, the newspaper he writes for back in Europe. In fact, he was the one who paid for his ticket to Australia, after Mr Mayseh wrote him such an impassioned letter. You would have known him as Rekhtman. They changed my name to Retter when I arrived in this country.'

Anna glanced across at Alter, whose face had turned pale.

'Yes, sadly, you will recall that my uncle died just before your arrival,' Retter continued.

'Oh. I'm so sorry, Mr Retter,' Anna said.

'No matter. He had been poorly for such a long time.' His eyes shone with warmth. 'And please, both of you, call me Leo.'

'Thank you, Leo.'

'Anyway, when Mr Mayseh finally arrived last spring, my aunt took my sister and me along to greet the boat. It was a brief encounter, and I had hoped to get to know him better, but after a couple of weeks our intrepid poet had already disappeared. Off on an adventure to explore this great country, I hear.'

'Well, there you have it!' Alter came up behind Leo Retter and slapped him on the back. 'We get to meet again, after all.'

'Your late uncle must have been a very generous man,' Anna said, trying to smooth over Alter's rough edges.

Leo sighed. 'Yes, indeed, he was. I also have him to thank for getting us out of Europe just in time. But I am very fortunate to still have my dear aunt. She has been like a mother to my sister and me since we arrived in Melbourne. It hasn't been easy, but we had an idea recently to start up a business making dolls.'

'Dolls?' Anna's eyes widened. 'I'd love to hear more.'

Alter hopped from one foot to the other, restless to leave. He placed a hand on Anna's shoulder, ushering her towards the entrance as he spoke.

'Well, my good man.' Alter looked back at Leo as he held the door open. 'It was lovely to see you again, but you'll have to excuse us. It is getting rather late, and I must see that Miss Winter gets home safely.'

'Oh, of course! I didn't mean to hold you up. It has been so wonderful to see you again.' He turned to Anna. 'And an honour to meet you, Miss Winter.'

As they strolled home, Anna prodded Alter. 'Why have you never told me you were so famous back home? That man, Leo, was so excited to meet you, I was half expecting him to bend down and kiss your feet.' She had been seated in the audience during the lecture, and although she hadn't understood more than a few words of what Alter had said, she had enjoyed watching the elated faces of those around her.

'Thank you for saving me from that little fellow. I felt so embarrassed I didn't know who he was.' Alter clucked his tongue.

'He seemed like a very kind man. You could have been a little more polite, especially since his uncle was your meal ticket over here.'

'Yes, yes. You're right. Maybe I should invite him out sometime.' He kicked some pebbles into the gutter. 'Anyway, to answer your question, let's just say there's not a lot of competition here as far as Yiddish writers go, so celebrity status is not that hard to come by. Whoever thought I would hear Yiddish spoken under the Southern Cross? There is that Waislitz. What a performer! An actor from the famous Vilna Troupe. He was a disciple of Stanislavski, who breathed life into Yiddish versions of Chekhov and Molière, and he is here on a world tour of thirty-seven one-man shows and performances. That fellow Goldhar from Lodz lives in Melbourne now – the first editor of a Yiddish newspaper here, a fine writer with an eye for detail, albeit tinged with darkness and a tincture of despair. And he tells me he has translated some of the local writers into Yiddish. I have even been invited to attend a performance of *The Dybbuk* in Melbourne's main theatre.'

'I've been meaning to ask you. What is a *dybbuk*?' Anna asked.

'That's what I spoke about in my lecture. It is a creature who lives between two irreconcilable worlds, a disembodied soul who wanders the face of the earth in a relentless search of a haven inside a living person.'

They walked on quietly for a while. Alter stopped suddenly in front of the entrance to the Carlton cemetery.

'Let's go inside,' he said.

'What for?'

'Maybe there's a *dybbuk* wandering around here I could introduce you to.' He smiled and kissed her.

'I thought you were taking me out for supper.'

'Believe me – this will be far more interesting, Anna. Just wait.' He led her past the entrance.

She followed him along the path, all the way over to the Jewish section. They walked along a row of gravestones.

'I want to show you something very interesting,' he said. See those symbols? They tell us about the people, who they were.'

'For example, this one over here.' He stopped in front of a grave. 'We can see he was a learned man by the symbol of holy books.' He pointed to two hands with thumbs joined, the fingers paired to form a V. 'These are *kohanim* hands, an ancient symbol of the priestly blessing. He must have been a *kohen*, a descendant of the priests of biblical Israel.'

They walked along the rows until they reached a gravestone with the image of a hand pouring water from a pitcher.

'This is a Levite. That means the person's ancestors were members of the Tribe of Levi, who assisted the priests by cleaning their hands.'

Beside it was a tiny grave, with a symbol of broken branches.

'A child?' Anna asked, stopping to read the inscription.

Alter nodded and walked away.

CHAPTER 25

CARLTON

JANUARY, 1939

Frischer Apfelkuchen – apple cake fresh from the oven. She had never been much of a cook, although she envied women who were. In Birdum she had learned to prepare the basics, but the clientele was hardly a fussy lot. She remembered her mother's recipe book, a culinary bible of neatly arranged perfect lines of script, one delicious dish to each page. Papa must have eventually packed it up and given it away, along with Mutti's dresses, shoes and coats. And with that, Anna had lost her mother all over again. Looking back, she felt as though he had been trying to hide his wife's very existence. The only piece of her clothing she had left was a strip torn from a red velvet scarf and knotted around Lalka's waist. As a child Anna would dig her nose into the fabric to try and elicit the feeling of comfort that her mother's scent brought back, holding onto an invisible thread between the worlds of the living and the dead.

There was a knock at the door. Even before she opened it, she could already feel Alter embracing her. She called from the hallway of her new house, where she lived alone now: 'Coming!'

She glanced in the mirror to check her lipstick. Alter stood at the front door, looking down at his feet. He was already as good as her husband; they had been a couple for almost a year now and a moment didn't go by where she didn't think of their future together. She had felt this day coming for a while. They spent all their free time in each other's company, and after the widow she had lived with died recently, he helped her move house, carrying furniture, books and boxes of dishes the family had kindly given her. The old lady had also left her a generous sum of money, which allowed Anna to rent her own place around the corner in Barkly Street.

Alter followed her into the dining room, where she had set the table – tea glasses, plum jam, sugar cubes, almonds, dried prunes, whipped cream.

'Sit down and make yourself comfortable. I'll just be a minute.'

She scurried to the kitchen and cut several pieces of cake, placing them on a blue plate that she brought back to the table.

'It's my first apple cake,' she said triumphantly. She felt her cheeks burn. 'My mother used to make this, only I never had the recipe.'

Her chatter bubbled over into his silence as he sat bent over, stabbing his fork into the heart of a slice. Crumbs scattered as he brought a piece to his lips. Her words tied themselves into loops, forming a giant knot in her stomach. He slurped his tea and tugged at his collar. Each time he opened his mouth, she waited expectantly for him to say something. Instead, he filled it with more cake. She couldn't bear it anymore. This shyness was so unlike him. He looked up at her for the first time since he had arrived.

She laughed. 'My darling, you are sweating.'

He sat there not moving, his face sullen.

'Let me make it easier for you.'

'No, Anna – you don't understand.'

'Oh, Alter. Is this how a poet proposes? I imagined it would be more like a gentle whisper from the midst of some ancient forest, or a giant roar from the depths of the ocean. You are even too nervous to make it a flea bite.' She laughed. 'Let me spare us both the agony.'

She smiled, placing another slice of cake on his plate, but he pushed it away this time. He stirred his tea, the clink of the spoon on the rim of the glass filling the sudden silence between them. He looked pale.

'What's wrong, Alter? Are you feeling ill?'

'No.' He wiped his brow. 'No.'

'Would you like me to say it for you?' She reached across the table, placing her hand on his. Her fingers searched for what she dreaded might already be lost. Like a prophet, she tried to divine the future from his palm, afraid she might find the line that designated a no-man's-land of his love.

He pulled his hand away as though he had been bitten by a snake. 'I really don't know how to say this.'

'I have something to tell you too, darling.'

He slid his chair back from the table and stood up, rubbing his throat as though he were trying to milk the words out. She had played out the scene of his proposal to her so many times in her head, but had never imagined he would have such stage fright. He walked across the room and stood facing the window, looking out onto the street. The bedroom door rested slightly ajar.

'Tell me, how many other messages are you hiding?' he asked quietly.

'Pardon? What are you talking about, Alter?'

He walked over to a shelf, picked up one of the dolls and carried it over to the table. It lay there on the tablecloth, smiling blandly at the ceiling. It was one of Anna's costume dolls – the Dutch girl.

'Let's see what's in this one, shall we?'

'I don't —'

Before she could finish her sentence, he picked it up and tore off the head.

'Alter!' she screamed. 'What are you doing?'

'How could you deceive me all this time?' he said angrily. He pulled out a small piece of paper from inside the doll's head and tossed it in front of her. 'There you have it. You have hoodwinked me all along – although was it betrayal when truth never really existed in the first place?' He looked up at her, the blue of his eyes rimmed with red. 'I've been such a fool. How did I not see it?'

'I don't understand.'

'Oh, but it's so clear now, Anna. I accidentally dropped one of your dolls this week when I was helping you move. The Spanish one, to be precise. And as I was trying to piece it together, I found a note – just like the one I pulled out of your Dutch doll just now. And there was one inside the Russian doll, too.'

He was glaring at her. She scanned his eyes, trying to understand, thinking perhaps she had misheard.

Then he uttered one short sentence that murdered their love: 'I would never have picked you for a Nazi.'

Words that burnt like fire. She had watched his mouth forming them, the tip of his tongue licking his cracked lips. A wave of nausea gripped her as she clutched her belly with one hand, grabbing the edge of the table with the other to steady herself. The tightly coiled silence grew between them. She looked away, falling into the chasm of purgatory that lay somewhere between her past and future. And with his words sank all her dreams – the sprawling marital bed, the desk on which he would write his poetry books, the pram she would wheel proudly around Carlton Gardens on weekends. Tears, laughter, arguments, dinners, desire, a family. *Their* family. She had lost the imagined life of ordinary people she had longed for. It had all vanished into the inky shadows in an instant.

She whispered his name. It was all she could offer in response – a question, a plea to explain, to erase what he had said, hoping he would smile and take her in his arms, saying it was all okay. But he stood there taciturn, his face shrouded with disgust.

'You used the dolls.'

'What are you talking about, Alter?'

'Those delightful messages from your darling Führer. I found them.' He reached into the inside pocket of his jacket and pulled out two small pieces of paper. Unfolding one, he read out loud in German: '*The largest threat to the Aryan is the Jew.*' He threw it on the table and read the other note: '*If the Jew conquers the world this planet will again move through the ether, devoid of humanity.*'

He lifted a small box from the pile in the hallway that Anna still hadn't unpacked. Opening it up, he pulled out the collection of tiny costume dolls she had brought with her from Germany.

Alter tipped the rest of the costume dolls onto the table. They lay sprawled out like a pile of bodies, with their sumptuous costumes of toile and velvet, a theatre of drama attached to each one. He picked up the Bavarian doll and, with a tug, forced its head off too. Anna sat there, horrified, unable to move or speak. He held the doll out to her. 'Look. Here is another one.' He read it out loud: '*With satanic lust, the black-haired Jewish youth lurks in wait for the unsuspecting Aryan virgin, defiling her with his blood and stealing her from her Volk.*'

With that, he picked up doll after doll and, like a triumphant executioner, tore off their heads, pulling out the yellowed notes from each one and throwing them onto the table. He ripped apart Egypt, Italy and Greece before destroying Uganda, New Zealand and Ecuador. He stood breathing heavily, clutching Scotland in his hand. Sparing the doll a similar fate, he lowered it back into the box.

'Each of these notes bears an uncanny resemblance to *Mein Kampf*. And all signed by Herr Hitler himself. Now I understand clearly why you never wanted to talk to me of your past. I don't know what the devil you were up to in Germany, but I sure as hell am not staying around to find out.'

'But Alter. I had absolutely no idea those notes were there.'

'You really expect me to believe that, Anna?' He turned to her. 'There's nothing left to say. I don't want you ever to come near me again.' Picking up his hat, he made his way to the front door and, without looking back, walked out of her life.

She felt she might drown in her own disbelief. Humiliation, disappointment, shame – all words too bland to describe the hot blade that had pierced her chest, carving her heart into small pieces. How could she have mistaken this hideous accusation for a marriage proposal? Yet how was she to explain something she could not even begin to fathom herself? Where had all these despicable notes come from? The emptiness of it all grew larger and larger, filling the room. Her head spun. She didn't understand. Had he tired of playing with her, like a morsel of prey tossed aside without even giving her a chance to defend herself? Drawing shallow breaths, she tried to stay afloat within the depths of panic and confusion.

Her wristwatch ticked away the moments that had passed since Alter closed the door quietly behind him and stepped out into the street. The notes lay on the table, spilling out from the dolls. The shadow of evening nibbled away at her, the day dissolving as she sat there shaking. His sudden departure had been a pathetic kind of violence. A knife would have been obvious, but his accusation had stabbed at the very soul of her being.

She should have seen it coming. How could she not have realised something was wrong? He had hardly uttered a word over the last few days. She felt the room might drop away, and with it the house, the wrought-iron gate, the footpath with its giant oak, the entire street – followed by St Patrick's Cathedral, the Royal Exhibition Building and the Kadimah Library where Alter spent so many of his days working to set up a Yiddish school. A huge crater would be left where his words had fallen like a bomb. She envied the headless dolls lying there. Their pain had been sudden, unlike the deep ache she was left carrying. She wanted to die holding sweet memories, not unfulfilled dreams.

Her hand trembled as she picked up one of the crumpled, yellowed notes and tried to read the tiny black scrawl. She reached for a magnifying glass and had to squint to make out the words: '*The Jew will stop at nothing. The devil himself takes on the living shape of the Jew. Lean years, but NSFM will soon rise again.*'

NSFM – the National Socialist Freedom Movement – it was the name the banned Nazi party had re-formed under, after Hitler's imprisonment in 1924. Her heart thrashed violently, stirring up the sediment of the past. Flashes of her childhood surfaced – Fraulein Schilling handing Papa a costume doll, Papa waiting outside in the car when Anna was taken to visit Hitler in Landsberg Prison, the professor whispering questions to Papa about the purity of Mutti's family. She'd always had suspicions as a child, perhaps even knew deep down whom she might be surrounded by – but that she,

Anna, could have been unwittingly drawn into this circle of evil back then? She began to glimpse what lay under the flimsy veil of childhood innocence.

It all became clear to her in an instant: the costume dolls had been used as a cover so the professor and his cronies could smuggle secret messages in and out of Landsberg Prison. After Hitler's arrest and the temporary demise of his party back in 1923, they had to go underground and were secretly regrouping, united by their aim to regain power. And Anna had been their unwitting child courier, smuggling the dolls that contained snippets of Hitler's vile manuscript out of the prison to be published. She was suddenly struck with a horrific thought. Had Papa known about this all along?

It made hideous sense now. How could she not have seen what was going on in front of her very eyes? But it was impossible to believe that her own sweet papa had been drawn willingly into this ghastly den of hatred and deception. Had this dear, loving man, who would do anything to protect her, truly been a Nazi? It would certainly explain a lot – Tantine's secret visits, all those weekends spent at Professor Jäger's house, Dr Magnussen's hideous experiments on those poor rabbits hidden away in the garden shed, the notes Fraulein Schilling secretly pulled out of the costume dolls. But surely it was impossible. Papa had always tried to protect her, shielding her from everything. And he was the one who had organised false papers for her and helped her escape. Professor Jäger himself had said Papa was misguided. She ran to the bathroom and hurled what felt like her very being into the basin. A wave of cramps gripped her belly like a vice. She felt something trickle down her leg and looked down to see a rivulet of blood on the tiled floor. Both her future and past had been horrifically despoiled.

After Alter left, and she lost the baby, Anna started to vanish. Not so much disappear as gradually fade away. She sat in the corner of the loungeroom surrounded by half-empty coffee cups and abandoned doll limbs. The torment oozed from every pore, hollowing her out. She opened her desk drawer and pulled out a photograph taken the day she and Alter met. Alter stood in front of the mail truck, grinning straight at the camera. Moments earlier, he had handed her the Box Brownie and run back to wedge himself between the Italian driver and his young Aboriginal guide. He smiled at her from across time, peering into the future through the camera lens, not knowing how powerfully his gaze would draw her in. She could still hear him call her name, but he stood beside her in memory only. Lalka watched from her place on the shelf.

CHAPTER 26

CARLTON

SUNDAY 3ʳᴰ SEPTEMBER, 1939

Anna sipped her tea as she sat by the radio, listening to the special evening broadcast.

'The following is an announcement from the Prime Minister Robert Menzies:'

'Fellow Australians, it is my melancholy duty to inform you officially that, in consequence of a persistence by Germany in her invasion of Poland, Great Britain has declared war upon her, and that, as a result, Australia is also at war.'

Her sleep was peppered with nightmares, Papa calling for her to run and hide in a forest haunted by evil spirits. The following morning, there was loud knock at the door.

'Open up!' The knocking continued.

Anna rushed down the hallway. Two armed police officers stood at the entrance.

'Miss Anna Winter?'

'Yes?'

They handed her a document. 'You are to accompany us to the station.'

'Why, officers? What have I done wrong?'

'Government orders, madam. All enemy aliens are to be arrested immediately.'

'Enemy aliens?'

'Yes. Those who are deemed to have possible links with the fascist regime in Europe, that is, from nations at war with Australia, and hence may pose a threat to the security of this country – including people of German or Austrian descent like yourself – are to be transferred to an internment camp until further notice.'

'But this can't be possible. I have been living in Australia for six years already and am a loyal citizen. Would you really strip me of any ounce of dignity I have left, just because of my nationality? I have done nothing wrong.'

'Sorry, madam. We don't make the rules.'

Papa always told her to be brave in all things. But lately, even navigating to and from work had become an ordeal. Australia's shores were meant to be free, a land where she could feel secure. How was she seen as an enemy alien after all she had been through? The gravity of war had reached far and wide. Nowhere seemed safe anymore. The whole idea of refuge, a hiding place from the monstrous winds of change, seemed futile now.

'Take a few minutes to pack a few personal items, but then I am afraid you will have to come along with us.'

She rushed to the bedroom, pulled Papa's old leather suitcase out from under the bed and threw in some clothes. She took Lalka down from the shelf and tucked her into her handbag. There was no way she was going to leave her treasured companion behind.

CHAPTER 27

TATURA INTERNMENT CAMP

JUNE, 1941

Almost two years had passed since the start of the war. Anna spent that time living behind barbed wire. Corrugated-iron huts were arranged row upon row, in military fashion, each one divided into two cabins by a masonite wall. They were raised off the ground, three wooden steps leading up to each entrance. Anna's cabin had its own window, a small table, two chairs and two bunks. Hooks nailed to the wall served as her makeshift wardrobe. Despite regular fumigation, lice were her constant companions. During the sweltering summers, she hung wet sheets across the doorway to try to cool the air down a little, but in winter, nothing could warm her up. Short, chilly days brought with them long, freezing nights. Every morning at dawn, without fail, the army bugler would wake all the internees, who tumbled out of their cots for morning roll call.

She was imprisoned at Camp Three, where internees came from all walks of life – doctors, musicians, teachers, tailors. A wide range of nationalities were represented, including Germans, Italians,

Japanese and even some people from New Zealand and Finland, of all places. Anna sometimes caught herself searching among the sea of faces, wondering if it might be possible that one of them was Max Schmidt. She had never heard what happened to him after he disappeared from Birdum.

So many people had vanished on this blood-swollen earth. She wondered if she would ever know the fate of those she had left behind. Was she deluded to think there might be any chance Papa was still alive somewhere? And as much as she told herself that she never wanted to lay eyes on Alter again, she couldn't help but wonder what had become of him.

Beyond the main living quarters lay a dam and acres of well-tended vegetable gardens, the pride of the internees. Just outside the barbed-wire fence, next to the main gate, a brick hut served as a temporary gaol for those who misbehaved. Not that anyone would find it easy to escape Tatura, which was too far from the coast to be much of a security concern. The gaol stood next to a large shed that housed a handicrafts and carpentry workshop.

Among the prisoners, all of them designated enemy aliens, were three hundred children, who attended school inside the camp all day, waiting impatiently for the highlight of the week, the Saturday evening puppet show. Karl Hennig, who had been a chef back in Vienna, set up Café Wellblech, with wooden tables and chairs arranged outside in the style of a European coffee house. He baked *Käsebrot* pastries in honour of the first puppet performance of the season. Official programmes were printed and distributed among the crowd, who mulled about excitedly in front of the makeshift theatre.

It was here that Anna ran into a familiar face.

'Anna?'

She looked up from her programme.

'Yes?'

'Leo. Leo Retter. Alter Mayseh introduced us after one of his lectures. My uncle was the one who brought him out to Australia.'

'Oh, yes! Of course, I remember.'

'What a coincidence meeting you here, of all places.'

'Well, it seems that it doesn't matter what your politics are, if you were born in the wrong place at the wrong time, you will end up here,' Anna said.

'Which part of the camp are you working in?'

'I'm helping out a little with the children.'

'We need a hand in the carpentry workshop. Would you like to join us making puppets for these performances? I remember you seemed quite interested in dolls the first time we met.'

It had been so long since Anna had felt even a flicker of excitement.

'Of course! I'd love to.'

During the long, strange months that followed, Anna worked side by side with Leo in the toy workshop. At first they hardly spoke, her bewildered reticence stifling most conversation. But gradually, she found herself opening up to him, surrounded by the watchful faces of handmade puppets and dolls. She told him things she had never shared with anyone. And he held out his hand to her before she even knew she needed it.

They called him Leo, although he much preferred his real name – Leopold.

'Is it so hard to pronounce?' he asked.

She laughed.

'Australians seem to break their tongues on anything more complicated than John Smith,' he said. 'So, Leopold Rekhtman became

Leo Retter, courtesy of the lazy customs official at Station Pier. At least he gave me the distinctive flourish of that double T in my new name, a creative highlight in what I imagine is the public servant's rather drab job.'

'My name has been changed too.'

'Really? What was it?'

'Müller. A good German name.'

They laughed about what other embellishments had been inflicted upon immigrants with unwieldy surnames, turning them bland for easier public consumption: Aarons becoming Ashton, Cohen vanishing under Cowan and Solomon hiding inside Sullivan.

'There is a joke doing the rounds about a Jewish man standing in line to be processed at the border entry,' Leo said. 'When his turn to present to the official came and he was asked his name, he felt so nervous that he stuttered and blurted out in Yiddish, *shoyn fargessen* – I've already forgotten. The clerk scribbled what he heard into a register and from then on, the man officially became known as Sean Ferguson.'

She was grateful that he didn't ask her more about her name. He was such a respectful man, knowing when not to pry.

When Leo had met Anna back in Melbourne, albeit a brief encounter, there was a strength and determination about her that he greatly admired. Yet here, in Tatura, where chance had tossed them together again, he noticed her hands were often bundled into fists, her voice a tiny bird's trill with a note of sadness.

One day as Anna carved a puppet's head, the small knife slipped from her hand, embedding itself in the pulpy flesh of her thumb. Leo leapt up from the workbench. Never one to be squeamish, he pulled out the blade and wrapped a strip of cotton material around her thumb, pressing the wound with his fingers to stop the bleeding. He sat her down on a chair and propped her arm up on cushions.

'You should have been a doctor,' she said, feeling a little faint.

Leo rinsed his hands and poured her a glass of water before he set about cleaning up the mess. The workbench looked like a scene from a horror movie.

When he finished he came and sat beside her.

'You need to be more careful, Anna.'

'Ha! Not one of my strengths, I'm afraid. I'm starting to feel I haven't anything left in me,' she said quietly.

She gave him a plaintive look and burst into violent sobs. She wept inconsolably, the dam wall she had kept intact all this time suddenly bursting. Years of agony and shame she had never spoken of to a soul came flooding out – Mutti's death, the professor's threats, Tantine's duplicity and, finally, Alter's accusations, which had left her wondering whether anything she had witnessed in her life had been real.

Leo sat quietly, listening to the torrent of nightmarish memories emerge. How had this woman contained it all for so long?

'I am not a Nazi, Leo. Please don't think that of me,' she pleaded, wiping tears away with the back of her wrist.

'Why would that even enter my head, Anna? For heaven's sake, you were a mere child growing up inside such a black cauldron of deception. I believe you.'

She calmed down a little. Numbness gave way to pain.

CHAPTER 28

CARLTON

1944

Anna had never imagined she would end up living and working with Leopold Retter. The week they were released from Tatura he invited her over for afternoon tea. Anna put on her best dress, pinned her hair up into a chignon and rouged her cheeks. When she arrived at his aunt's house, where he was staying with his younger sister Zelda, she was greeted warmly.

'My nephew has told me so much about you, Miss Winter,' the elderly lady held out her hand. 'Come sit with us.'

On the sideboard was a photo of Leo and Zelda as children, seated side by side in a little wooden cart pulled along by two billy goats. Leo noticed her looking at it.

'We used to love spending time in the park in Vienna,' he said. 'It was just around the corner from our house.'

Zelda poured some tea and slid a plate of biscuits towards Anna. 'Some *Vanillekipferl*? I baked them myself.'

Leo had told Anna that when he and Zelda first arrived, his

elderly aunt, who had come to Melbourne with her husband in 1926, was there to greet them on the dock.

'Where are all the people?' he had asked his aunt as they walked around Carlton later that day.

'That's the beauty of this country,' she had replied. 'There's space to breathe.'

On his first evening in Melbourne, he had stood out in the backyard of her old weatherboard house in Leicester Street and looked up at the giant ring of light surrounding a full moon.

Back in Vienna Leo had worked in films, but when Nazi-inspired regulations called for Jews to be banned from the industry, he knew it was time to flee. He would find somewhere in the world where he could build a new career. Luckily, his uncle and aunt were able to sponsor both teenagers to come out to Australia and they escaped just in time. They had heard from various sources that the rest of the family had not been so lucky, although they had so far been unable to confirm this gruesome news.

'We must work hard to make this our home,' Leo had said to Zelda. 'We'll stitch together our lives and create something new. You'll see.'

Soon after their arrival Leo took over a dusty corner of his aunt's shed, clearing away the cobwebs, which were adorned with shrivelled cockroach carapaces. This would become a dreamer's cave. A broom swept away sorrow, clearing space for optimism and wonder. He would create a business built on smiles and love. But with the outbreak of war, and his sudden internment at Tatura, everything had to be put on hold.

Leo was an obstinate man: once he made his mind up, nothing would stop him. He knew that war could also bring with it strange opportunities. Imports of German and Japanese dolls had already been drying up in Australia. His idea was to produce a perfect prototype for a doll's head on which to model all the others, and start a successful homegrown doll workshop.

Leo put down his teacup. 'Anna,' he said, clearing his throat, 'Let's get straight to the point, shall we? We want you to help us set up a doll factory in Carlton.'

Anna smiled. 'That's very kind of you, sweet man, but I'm afraid I hardly have enough money even for lodgings, let alone a large venture like that.'

Leo smiled. He held out his hand. 'Come with me. I want to show you something.'

He led her to the garage where he was building his world of dolls.

'I want you to be part of all this, Anna. How would you like to come live with us and we can all work on the project together?'

'That's such a lovely gesture,' she said.

Leo was a true gentleman, who lived life without the embellishment of quixotic dreams. She accepted his offer to move in, finally determined to throw off any wistful memories of Alter. It wasn't long before he proposed to her and she heard herself say 'yes'. Love didn't need to be fiery and breathless. She had found warmth and trust instead.

They married in a simple civil service at the Births, Deaths and Marriages Registry in town one Thursday afternoon, with Leo's aunt and his sister Zelda as their witnesses. Anna wore a beige skirt and cream silk blouse, and carried a small bouquet of daphne.

They had already been married several months when Leo came into the workshop after breakfast one day, cradling Lalka gently like a child.

Anna smiled. 'What are you doing? I thought we agreed we weren't going to have children?'

'I know, Anna. It's not that,' he said. 'I've been thinking. What if we used Lalka as a model to create our own prototype doll.'

If there was one thing Germans knew how to do, aside from decimate an entire continent, it was how to make fine dolls. Up until the outbreak of war, the sheer quantity of dolls produced there placed them at the forefront of the world doll market. But this golden age had been ended by the economic recession. This was where Leo saw such enormous opportunity.

Anna sat quietly, listening to his idea.

'She would be our inspiration for our most popular doll.'

Leo seemed feverish with excitement. If they were able to mass-produce her, the Australian version of Lalka – a classic Waltershausen doll made by J.D. Kestner – she would become the special doll that every little girl longed for.

'Yes,' Anna smiled. It felt oddly right.

They placed Lalka on the table. She sat up, arms outstretched, staring back at them. Laying out pages of old newspaper, Anna carefully peeled off Lalka's clothes.

'It's okay,' Anna told Lalka. 'You're going to be quite a famous doll soon.'

Even though Leo had recreated himself as a toymaker, read all the books and signed up for newsletters from international doll enthusiast clubs, he still found dolls a bit unnerving. They were little creatures holding invented, oversized personalities.

'Yes, it's okay, Lalka. Sit still.' He found himself talking to the doll too, as if she were their child, gently applying wet newspaper to her cheek.

He dipped a paintbrush into a pot and smeared some glue onto the paper, applying more in turn. He tore tiny strips to mould around the thin lips, but the soggy layers kept falling off. He was intent on finding the right shape that might please children enough for a doll to earn their love. Anna held Lalka as he worked. When he was done, he cleaned Lalka's face, put her clothes back on and carefully returned her to Anna's arms. Leo ran his fingertips over the mask, smoothing out the wet mush.

That night, Anna lay in bed, Lalka watching her in the dark. She reached out and pressed the doll to her chest, burying her face into Lalka's hair. The smell of glue seeped into her nostrils. The Mutti scent was gone, the faint memory of delphiniums and roasted chestnuts replaced by an acrid odour of fixative. Stifling a wave of regret, she cried herself to sleep. In dreams she shrugged off the world, riding the crest of memories that swept her onto the shores of the past and into its murky depths. Yet an imaginary future teased her with rays of hope. When daybreak flooded in through the flimsy curtains she awoke to the here and now, determined to embrace her life with resolve.

CHAPTER 29

CARLTON

TUESDAY 6TH JUNE, 1944

Anna was required to carry her travel permit with her at all times. Dated 3 NOV 1943, the national security card screamed at her accusingly – *GERMAN. Enemy Alien.*

> *Permit: From date of issue until cancelled or reviewed.*
> *Purpose: to travel to her place of employment at L. J. Retter & Co.,*
> *Carlton, and to move freely for business and recreational purposes*
> *within 15 miles of the G.P.O. Melbourne. And to report once a*
> *month to the Police.*
> *Signed by the Aliens Registration Officer.*

Their radio had been confiscated, so she had to rely on what she overheard or saw on the front page of Leo's newspaper. The day's headlines shouted: *BOMBERS SWOOP ON RETREATING GERMANS.* Over 150,000 Allied troops had stormed the beaches of Normandy overnight, attacking Nazi Germany. The newspaper reported it as one of the greatest military operations in history, with thousands dying during the attack. She felt like a moth who had managed to escape a giant spider's web. The grandfather clock cried out the time. It was a massive mahogany antique given to Leo by a customer who had died a lonely death. Oppressive in its precision, on the hour it hammered out a bittersweet reminder of time passing. It had just sounded five o'clock when she heard Leo climbing the stairs from the workshop. Anna was sitting at the kitchen table, eyes half-closed.

Leo had been so kind to her, making sure she always had enough to eat, bringing her bowls of soup and schnitzels with mashed potatoes for lunch. Together they were learning the tricks of the doll trade. The L. J. Retter doll factory was Anna's centre of gravity now, keeping her tethered to life. Leo had been issued with a permit from the Department of War Organisation of Industry to order machinery for the mass production of his dolls. Now he had found a prototype, he could go ahead and place the order.

Leo sat opposite, lifting the newspaper from the table.

'Have you seen the headlines? It looks like the war may be over soon. There's finally some hope.'

Anna nodded distractedly.

'I've changed my mind.' Anna said.

He peered over the top of the page. 'About what?'

'About what we're doing to Lalka.'

He folded the newspaper and placed it on the chair beside him.

She cradled her face in her palms and suddenly started sobbing uncontrollably.

'Anna, what's wrong?'

'We're ruining her,' she bawled.

'Oh, no, darling. I didn't mean to upset you. I only wanted to honour you and Lalka, and the memory of your dear mutti.' He got up and made his way over to her, gently placing his hands on her shoulders.

'I know that, but Lalka has been my rock since I was a young girl.' Anna calmed down a little as Leo wiped her tears with his handkerchief. 'You might be able to copy her face,' she said, 'but I don't want you to use her name.'

'Okay, that isn't a problem at all. Let's call our new doll Lorraine instead, with Lalka as our inspiration. Believe me, every doll in Australia will be jealous of her, and all the little girls will be lucky enough to have their very own Lalka – or Lorraine – to love. She has been such a wonderful friend to you. Every girl deserves to have such a loyal companion.'

Within a few weeks dozens of Lorraines were lined up in the workshop, each one wearing an identical bride's dress with silver trimming on the sleeves. Lorraine would be every little girl's dream, manifest as a doll. She could act out the imagined union over and over as she waited for her groom to arrive.

Anna preferred to work alone. For one thing, there were no clients hovering over her. Leo sat in his cramped office at the back of the warehouse, surrounded by files and doll samples. They had an unspoken understanding – he was available if she had any questions, but would never dream of intruding on her workspace without asking. Except on Fridays. That was the day he spent dusting and cleaning, not trusting anyone else with their precious dolls. When they first started the company Leo had given Anna a pair of gloves, which she promptly set aside. She wasn't sure if he had meant the gift to protect the dolls from getting dirty, or to save Anna's hands, all red and peeling. But she never wore them; gloves formed a barrier between her and the doll.

Carefully opening a box that held a new doll, Anna felt as though she were a small child again, unscathed and hopeful. But as an adult her eye was keener, and she saw her own demons reflected in the doll's eyes. Dolls could bend in any direction, their pliable, impossible bodies performing skilled acrobatics like circus performers. Designed to mimic all the distortions of anatomy and the false promise of eternal life, they made a mockery of the delicate tightrope of vulnerability human beings balanced upon.

The intricacy of artificial eyelashes, matched by the coiffure of repurposed human hair, the careful carving of wooden teeth outlined with pink rosebud lips that never uttered a word – the workshop was a panoply of lifelike dolls who lived in the bardo of human creation and assembly. They existed in gelatinous time, a glimpse into the past, and the legacy of childhood. Late at night, inside an opera of silence, Anna often felt Lalka was simply masquerading as a doll, alive among them all. The oozing of glue trailing along the joins between her limbs and torso turned to blood in the uncertain boundary of dreams.

'You know something?' Leo asked, stopping in front of Anna as she sat tinkering with a tiny broken shoe. 'I'm angry too.'

He stood facing her, this garden gnome of a man, a permanent smile imprinted on his rotund face. He scrunched a rag up into a ball, torn from one of his old shirts. Nothing went to waste at L. J. Retter & Co. He had spent the past hour carefully dusting the shelves in the workshop.

'The world doesn't owe us anything, Anna.'

She looked at the back of his hands, dotted with tiny brown islands, blue veins bulging under wrinkled skin. She watched him moving along the rows of dolls, taking his time as he polished the face of each one. He opened the cabinet where those he had built himself were kept. Some were perfect, others only models, the rough prototypes for what was to become a line of dolls loved by children around Australia. Yvonne, Janette and Lorraine, his brides, had long veils stitched onto their curly hair. Each of them wore a uniquely designed lace frock and clutched a tiny bouquet of flowers in one hand. The other hand reached out, inviting an invisible groom to lead them to the altar.

'Is part of you still in love with him?' he asked.

'Who?'

'You know who I am talking about.'

'No, Leo. Of course not. Why would you even think that after everything I have told you? How could I ever love someone who accused me of being a Nazi sympathiser?'

True. Alter had been cruel to treat her the way he had, jumping to the very worst of conclusions and not even trying to piece together the mystery behind the notes inside the dolls.

'Sometimes people just toss dolls into the rubbish, but doll-makers like us know they can be repaired,' Leo said. 'It's the marriages of parts that are more difficult to fix, those dolls brought in stitched together with ill-fitted heads and unmatched limbs hidden under elaborate costumes. Strange compositions tucked away under a veneer of gentility.'

He moved towards the workbench and stood beside her. She looked up.

'Aren't we all a bit like that, Anna?' He stroked her cheek. 'Patchwork people, thrown together in a jumble of ancestry. Who knows what our true origins are? For all you know, your mother might have been Jewish – perhaps that's what your papa was trying to hide in order to protect you? And maybe way back, someone in my own family was a Jew-hater. What does it matter now, as long as we don't carry the sediment of hatred in our blood? Surely there is enough of that in this world?' He blushed and cleared his throat. 'Well, I'd better leave you alone now.'

'Thank you, my dearest.' Anna said as he headed towards the door. 'For all you have done.'

Some of the dolls had sagged into themselves over time, almost toppling over. Anna saw them all as if for the first time, the lonely years they marked off, their owners who had once cradled them with loving arms now grown or gone. She picked up an Yvonne doll and felt a sudden urge to throw her across the room, smashing her papier-mâché skull, enraged by the eternal waiting for Mr Right. Then she would turn on Janette and Lorraine, smashing each one against the back of her chair before hurling them over to where Yvonne lay. On top of this carnage of brides Anna would pile beach girls in frilly bathing suits and angelic babies wearing pretty organdie outfits with pink trim. She imagined herself standing amid the wreckage, surrounded by a sea of shattered dolls.

Her heart racing, she opened the bottom drawer of her desk and pulled out a book of Spinoza's poetry that Alter had given her. He had been translating it into Yiddish at the time they met. She opened its pages and a photo fell out – the moment of their first meeting captured in a faded image. She never wanted to look at it again, Alter's face filled with adventure and promise. She had lied to Leo just now. The Yiddish poet was still there in everything she did; in the air around her, even as she rushed past the kosher butcher on Lygon Street, remembering how he would dry-retch at the sight or smell of meat. She tore up the photo and threw the pieces in the bin. Some dried-out native flowers he had once picked for her in Birdum fell out of another page, crumbling into dust.

Alter had said he loved her. Cried that he longed for them to be together forever, could never have written the kind of poetry he had until she came along. And even though the dream had been poisoned, yes, somewhere inside she still stupidly loved him. The words that had roared past his lips when he showed her the notes he had found in her dolls haunted her: *I would never have picked you for a Nazi.* Even when she had heard them, she had still somehow believed he would stay with her. He was a man who would be prepared to sacrifice everything for the sake of his art, and she had been his most powerful muse.

Anna stared at the row of perfect Lorraine brides, who would spend both winter and summer hibernating, year after year, waiting to know the body of a man, benign smiles pressed on their faces like prophecies of what was to come. But behind their uniform visage, she saw her very own Lalka. In her mind Anna slowly began to sweep up the carnage of dolls she had just pretended to destroy. The Lorraines watched her as she stared back at them indignantly. Lalka, stripped of her uniqueness, her history forgotten, was now moulded into a model Australian girl.

CHAPTER 30

CARLTON

1949

The doll workshop was sandwiched between a run-down milk bar and a denture clinic. Office workers wearing long overcoats rushed past like shadows. On the other side of the dusty front window a silhouette sat hunched over the workbench, repairing a doll.

Anna heard the insistent knocking, even though the sign on the door said OPEN. She knew never to get up too soon. Whoever it was would eventually realise the door was unlocked. A customer needed time alone with their own memories before they approached her with the business of what they thought they had come in for. The job itself was never that important: a doll could usually be cured, at least the older ones. Yeti, her lazy cat, sat in a box of discarded plastic doll limbs, licking his white fur. The latest models of dolls seemed to be manufactured to fit in with a growing throwaway lifestyle, one in which newer was always better. They cracked easily along visible seams left over from the moulds of their mass production. Hair now made from strings of nylon instead of wool from Angora goats, or real human hair for the high-end dolls, made them safety hazards for children, too. Dolls were supposed to provide refuge from the daunting world of adults, Anna mused. She repaired dolls, but felt that her real job was to give people back their childhoods by restoring hidden memories – to help people find what they didn't even realise was missing. What people nowadays didn't seem to understand was that dolls have always taken much more care of their owners than the owners have of them. Like Lalka, who had been her constant companion – more trustworthy, more reliable than many of the people in Anna's life.

The knocking finally stopped and the bell tinkled, the wooden door opening into a theatre of frozen faces that stared at the customer from every angle. Brides dressed in white lace, babies in crocheted cardigans and bonnets, and teddy bears with floppy ears lined the shelves and tables or sat propped up in baskets and miniature wicker prams. Antique dolls rested in a special glass cabinet tucked away in the corner of the room, seated neatly in a row on each shelf. Sweet painted smiles invited visitors to enter the lair and, once inside, trapped them inside the wilds of their childhood.

She was eager to close for the day and go upstairs to start pre-paring dinner, but she kept working on Betty, fitting her head back onto her body now that her eye had been replaced. Seated at her worktable, Anna could hear the heavy steps of the customer as he walked around the shop, his initial loud guffaws and laughter ebbing away into tiny sobs he attempted to disguise by coughing. She let him seek her out, waiting quietly until he stood beside her, clearing his throat like a child trying to gain the attention of its mother. Glancing up, Anna could see he was young and wiry with a head of wild, straw-coloured curls. His belt was drawn tight around a pair of baggy trousers; he looked like he hadn't eaten a decent meal in a while.

'Good evening.' He spoke with a familiar accent.

She cleaned a final dab of glue from Betty's eye and stood up slowly, reaching to place the doll on a wooden shelf beside the workbench.

'Would you like some help?' The young man reached out his hand.

'No!' She shielded the porcelain head with her body. 'I can do it myself, thank you.'

She turned around, glaring at the overzealous fellow, and suddenly felt faint. It was impossible. The twilight visitor looked just like – but no, it couldn't be. Years had gone by; surely he would have aged since then? Besides, she had heard he had moved to Montreal soon after they – well, no, she must be confused, overtired, seeing things. She rubbed her eyes.

'We are just about to close.'

A gentle voice floated over the top of the dolls' heads. 'The sign says you're still open.'

Right on cue, the bell announced someone else walking in off the street.

The blond man turned and beckoned his friend over. 'Menachem. Hello! Come in, come in.'

A short man with a smiley round face limped towards them.

'He insists on buying me a going-away present,' the scrawny one told Anna, patting his friend on the back. 'A *tchatchke* for the journey.'

'I want that he should have something to remember me by,' the short man said, taking off his hat as he smiled at Anna. He waved his hand around, pointing at the dolls. 'He loves all this junk. I told him he'd make more *parnose*, a good living, if he stuck to Australian landscapes – they're very popular here and are worth a lot more money. But no. He is a poor artist, obsessed with painting broken dolls and rusty toys.'

The blond man snorted. 'Haven't I told you a hundred times not to call me an artist? I'm a painter. I get up every morning and I *shmeer*. Painting is a profession, a real job. An artist is nothing more than a *flotser* – all wind.'

'I know, I know. And that is why you're always broke, Yosl.'

Yosl poked out his tongue, like a child.

'So, choose something already,' Menachem said, feigning exasperation.

The chatty blond man picked up a dusty old toy.

His friend laughed. 'Of all the things in this shop, that's what you want? An old nodding, wooden donkey? That's the thing you'll remember me by Yosl when you've become a famous artist – sorry – painter? *Narisher mentsh*. I always knew you were a little crazy.'

'And you, Menachem, I'll remember you for that time Frankie Simons made a wager with Jimmy Dolianatis that you wouldn't be able to swim across the Murray. Every soldier in Tocumwal came out to place their bets that day. And you, my little friend, Menachem, *mit der krume foos*, made it, despite your crooked foot! *Polio-shmolio*. You were a real champion that day!'

Tiny heads lined the shelf beside Anna's workbench; small arms and legs lay scattered. Yosl pointed to them. 'They look almost human, don't they?'

His brilliant blue eyes stared right through her, across time and place. The ache she felt was sudden and unexpected, as though she had been stabbed in the chest. His face disappeared into a sepia wash of memory. Even the way he spoke was the same.

'Like small *golems*,' he added.

Here he was, himself a kind of *golem* brought to life, right before her eyes. Anna watched him as he wandered around the showroom, his hands reaching out to touch only the strangest and most forlorn among the toys and dolls.

'Where are you going?' she asked.

'Away.'

'Isn't that where everyone goes?'

'I'll be attending art school in Montreal. I have a dear uncle living there, who is sponsoring me. He was quite an adventurer in his day; used to live in Australia for a while. He is quite a well-known Yiddish poet nowadays. Maybe you have heard of him?'

'Alter Mayseh,' she said. Just speaking the name out loud made her shiver.

'Ha! How did you know?'

'You look just like him.'

'That's what everybody tells me. They say we have the same blue eyes.' He placed his finger on the wooden donkey's head, making it nod. 'You knew him? That's incredible. Sadly, he is very ill – he had a weak heart his whole life, but it finally gave way. The doctors don't know how long he has left. A natural coward, but also capable of crazy acts of courage.' He spoke of Alter in the past tense, as if he were already dead. 'High drama, day and night. You know, when I was a child back in Radymno he used to disappear for months on end, always returning with exciting tales of his travels filled with adventure and danger – which none of us ever believed, of course. He saved my life bringing me out to Australia just in time, but soon ran off to Canada, leaving me here all alone.'

'Not exactly alone,' Menachem slapped him on the back.

Anna felt parts of herself clicking into place, put together and reassembled like a toy. To be given a second chance and poured into a new mould, emerging freshly minted with no indentations or scars. Unbreakable now. She wouldn't give up. She had been ripped apart like some despicable creature, but Leo had saved her from the scrap heap, scooping her up and giving her a job, a roof over her head and undying love. But the murmuring inside her never stopped. Some days she had no choice but to collaborate with the crumbling dead, as they rustled beneath her feet like dry leaves blown by an ill wind wherever she trod. They whispered their pleasure that she had returned to them, calling her quietly to join them.

She sat still, steeped in her own memories. Searching the young man's face, she finally made peace with all that she had lost.

'By the way, how did you know my uncle?' he asked.

'We were acquaintances.'

Yosl stared at her as she spoke. He didn't seem to be listening to what she said, or to care much about her answer. 'You have such unusual eyes. They are hauntingly beautiful. Would you let me paint your portrait?'

'Me? I am nothing but a rotting ghost.'

'Ha! All the better for me.' He smiled. 'Ghosts are impenetrable to decay. Besides, I am the heir to an entire family of phantoms. They don't frighten me anymore.'

His friend Menachem limped over to them. 'So, Yosl. What will it be?'

Yosl reached up quickly and lifted Lalka down from the shelf. 'I like this old doll very much,' he laughed. 'She has a lot of character.'

Menachem pulled out a five-pound note from his pocket. 'How much?'

'Give that back.' Anna glared at the young man. 'She's not for sale.' She reached out to grab Lalka back.

'What can I do? The crazy *meshugene* likes to paint pictures of *tsekrochene*, broken old toys that he collects,' Menachim said, throwing another five-pound note down in front of her. 'And not only that. He loves to draw junk – rusty old graters, lamps. He's an eccentric, but I'm going to miss him when he's gone. Livens things up around here, you know.'

'I told you,' Anna pushed the money back towards them. 'She's not for sale.'

'No, no! It's okay. I'll take the donkey instead.' Yosl looked at Anna and smiled, returning Lalka back to her place on the shelf. 'We'll leave this one here where it belongs. *Yede hartz hot soydes.*'

Every heart has its secrets.

EPILOGUE

CARLTON

1949

Anna locked the front door and turned the sign around: CLOSED. She'd had enough of customers today, with their endless complaints, spilling out their life stories and dreadful woes uninvited. She did not want to be the mender of souls, nor the repairer of broken dreams. She was there to fix dolls, not hearts.

Betty sat on the shelf, her new blue eye repaired, a perfect match. Anna had told the woman to collect her doll just before closing, but it was already five o'clock and Betty's owner still hadn't appeared. She had obviously forgotten about it. Funny how clients were always in a hurry to have their dolls fixed, but when asked to come back later because she didn't want to be rushed, it inevitably took them several days to return. If they ever did. She wiped down the workbench and cleaned her tools. Lalka sat watching Anna gather up assorted limbs and body pieces and place them in a tub labelled 'Spare Parts', which she slid under the bench. Then she gently dropped the tangle of eyes – green, blue and brown glass orbs, threaded onto the ends of a thin wire – into a silk-lined wooden box. She looked up at her favourite doll, her life companion, and thought about how far they had travelled together, how much Lalka had witnessed over the years, holding all Anna's secrets.

'*Always look behind the eyes for truth*,' Papa had told her.

Lalka seemed to be winking at her. Anna packed up her things, threw a shawl around her shoulders and hung the keys on a hook by the door. Betty was propped up on a shelf, at the end of a row of dolls. Once a month, Anna had started taking all these repaired dolls, abandoned by customers, over to a Jewish orphanage. It was filled with young children who had lost their families during the war. Some of them had no one left in the world. They had been brought from Europe to Australia by boat, sponsored by a couple who had no children of their own.

Anna had already taken off her laboratory coat and hung her bag over her shoulder, ready to go upstairs, when something made her look up at Lalka again. She noticed that the doll's left eye appeared strangely off centre. In all these years, despite being carted around the world, Lalka had never needed any sort of repair. She was a survivor, stronger and far more resilient than any of the newer models. Anna reached up and took Lalka down from the shelf, resting her on the table. Her blue eye was sitting at a weird angle, looking outward, as if she had a squint.

It had been a long day, and Anna was tired. She still needed to make it to Polonski's on Lygon Street to pick up some chops for dinner. But that eye bothered her. It wasn't right. She put her bag on the end of the bench and sat down on her stool again. She lay Lalka on her back and, following the same steps she had learned from Fraulein Schilling in the Puppetarium all those years ago, went about carefully removing the doll's head so she could check the faulty eye.

Lalka lay there decapitated as Anna searched her box for an eye that would perfectly match the original. She had just turned her attention back to the doll when she noticed a piece of yellowed paper poking out from inside her head, in the small space that lay behind the eye socket. It was rolled up into a miniature scroll. She felt a sudden wave of terror.

Using a pair of fine forceps, she carefully prised the paper out and slowly unrolled it. There were tiny letters scrawled on it. A note, or a letter of sorts, longer than the ones Alter had found inside her costume dolls. Years later, she still recognised her father's writing. Trembling, she grabbed her magnifying glass and started to read:

My darling Anna. I have always told you truth lies behind the eyes. When you read this, it's likely I will be long gone. No matter what it may seem, everything I have done in my life has been to shield you from harm. Sadly, there are people in this world who deplore anyone who is different. But there are always those who resist them like Mutti and me, and dearest Fraulein Schilling. Together, we prevented many of Hitler's vile ideas reaching publication. The dolls doubled as our couriers. I know you have witnessed far too much pain for a young girl. Your eyes are so beautiful and wise – when you look upon things, may you see where real love and truth lie. I am ready to leave this world so that you might live freely. But I will watch over you forever. Love, Papa.

She pictured him standing before her, his strong face and gentle eyes, and saw him clearly now. He had lived in a private world of his own all those years, his allegiance to the Resistance hidden behind his mundane job as a chauffeur. A double life.

He had always told her: '*Sometimes it is easier not to look at things we do not wish to see.*'

Just then, Leo came in through the back door, followed closely by a young girl, who ran straight over to Anna.

'Mama!'

Anna lifted the child onto her lap. 'Rachel, my sweetheart. Have you been having fun with Daddy?'

Leo came up to hug them both. 'Anna, darling. Surely that's enough work for today. You need to rest. I've put on a pot of soup.' He stopped short, seeing Lalka splayed open on the workbench.

Anna picked up the letter and handed it to him. He took time to read and then, resting his glasses on his forehead, reached out and hugged his wife and child. Anna looked up at him, this man who had saved her from darkness. His eyes were filled with tears.

'Mama,' Rachel said, clutching her mother's hand. 'What happened to Lalka?'

Leo and Anna both looked at their little daughter. She was only seven years old, an orphan from Germany they had adopted from the Jewish Refugee Children's Home, but she had seen things during the war no child should have to witness.

'Her eye is broken,' Anna said.

'Will she ever be able to see again?'

'Of course, darling. You can help me fix her tomorrow. Then, if you like, she can become your doll.' She bent down and kissed her young daughter's cheek. 'Lalka will always be there to look out for you.'

In memory of the Roma and Sinti children whose eyes were cruelly harvested for Dr Karin Magnussen's experiments in Aryanisation, under the direction of Dr Josef Mengele, at the concentration camp of Auschwitz during the regime of the Third Reich.

Magnussen died in 1997 aged eighty-nine in a nursing home in Bremen, having evaded prosecution for her war crimes. Mengele eluded his captors for thirty-four years, escaping to South America. He drowned in 1979 while living in Brazil.

ACKNOWLEDGEMENTS

I am indebted to so many people who have helped in the writing of this book. Special thanks to Yangman elders David Daniels and Robin Johns and their Welcome to Country and guidance during the research phase, and to Damien Singh of the Katherine Regional Council for his assistance.

I am grateful for the generosity and vision of my mentor and friend, the late Yosl Bergner, who first introduced me to his father Melekh Ravitch's quixotic imaginings back when I was a teenager.

My publisher at Penguin Random House, Meredith Curnow, is nothing short of brilliant (and patient), as are her team – editor Rachel Scully, designer Debra Billson and proofreader Katie Purvis. My thanks also to Bella Arnott-Hoare in publicity and Rebekah Chereshsky in marketing. I am grateful to my wonderful agent Peter Straus, of RCW Literary Agency, who believed in this book from the start. And to Louise Ryan, who championed *Doll's Eye* from that very first cuppa.

Generous and talented writer–friends Meg Keneally, Alice Nelson and Toni Jordan have helped me craft my nascent ideas into a finished book.

My dear friend Alice Nelson introduced me to the Doll Museum in L'Isle-sur-la-Sorgue, France, where the first idea for this book was born. Together with Professor Gh'ilad Zukermann, she then accompanied me on a quest to find the remains of the town Birdum. I acknowledge the invaluable assistance of Lauren Reed from the Katherine Museum who showed me the 'Planetarium' truck, and Anne Weerdenburg at the Doll Hospital in Melbourne who taught me so much about the world of dolls. Along the way, I have been lucky enough to have the support of Eileen and Peter Jacobs, Garry Disher, Peter Bishop, Antoni Jach, Jacinta Halloran, Catherine Therese, Rev. Barbara Allen, Delia Falconer, David Carlin, Robin Hemley, Danny Shub, Pam Maclean, Tom Keneally, Bram Presser, Suzanne Leal, Clint McCown and Ondra Hadras of the Pink Panther Hotel in Larrimah, Northern Territory.

Very early musings appeared in *Griffith Review*, thanks to Ashley Hay and Julianne Schultz. My deepest gratitude to the wonderful Alexia Holt and her team at Cove Park, Scotland, for a Writers' Fellowship in 2022, courtesy of the Bridge Awards and Varuna, the National Writers' House of Australia. Special thanks to Veechi Stuart. *A sheynem dank* to Dr Nathan Wolski at the Australian Centre for Jewish Civilisation, Monash University, for checking my Yiddish spelling.

Where would I be without my dear friends Donna-Lee Frieze, Diana Hanaor, Deborah Leiser-Moore, Lee Kofman, Daryl Karp, Lisa Berryman, Julie Lustig, Ewan Burnett, Brendan Higgins and Renelle Joffe, who have held my hand along the way?

My family – Ella, Maia, Alon and Yohanan Loeffler – have lived and breathed *Doll's Eye* since its inception, and are my true co-authors and greatest supporters.

Also by Leah Kaminsky

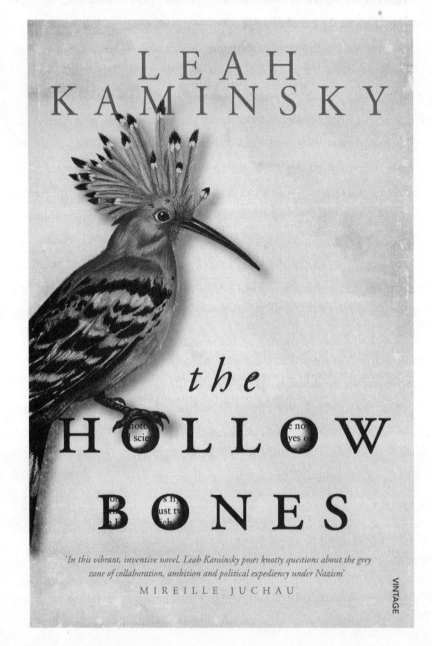

LEAH
KAMINSKY

the
HOLLOW
BONES

*'In this vibrant, inventive novel, Leah Kaminsky poses knotty questions about the grey
zone of collaboration, ambition and political expediency under Nazism'*
MIREILLE JUCHAU

VINTAGE

'I remember you once told me about mockingbirds and their special talents for mimicry. They steal the songs from others, you said. I want to ask you this: how were our own songs stolen from us, the notes dispersed, while our faces were turned away?'

Berlin, 1936. Ernst Schäfer, a young, ambitious zoologist and keen hunter and collector, has come to the attention of Heinrich Himmler, who invites him to lead a group of SS scientists to the frozen mountains of Tibet. Their secret mission: to search for the origins of the Aryan race. Ernst has doubts initially, but soon seizes the opportunity to rise through the ranks of the Third Reich.

While Ernst prepares for the trip, he marries Herta, his childhood sweetheart. But Herta, a flautist who refuses to play from the songbook of womanhood and marriage under the Reich, grows increasingly suspicious of Ernst and his expedition.

When Ernst and his colleagues finally leave Germany in 1938, they realise the world has its eyes fixed on the horror they have left behind in their homeland.

A lyrical and poignant cautionary tale, *The Hollow Bones* brings to life one of the Nazi regime's little-known villains through the eyes of the animals he destroyed and the wife he undermined in the name of science and cold ambition.

'From the horrors and dark truths of the Reich, Kaminsky fashions a poignant romance within a chilling, mesmerising narrative.'
Carmel Bird

...take of adventure, competing loyalties and the folly of sacrificing reason on the ideological altar.'
Bram Presser

Discover a
new favourite